STONE BABY

Stories

Michelle Sacks

TriQuarterly Books
Northwestern University Press
Evanston, Illinois

TriQuarterly Books
Northwestern University Press
www.nupress.northwestern.edu

An earlier, shorter version of "Kingdom" appeared in *New Contrast* 41, no. 3.
An earlier, slightly different, and shorter version of "Wurden wir mit dem Leben
belohnt oder bestraft?" called "Man Dies Alone" appeared in *African Pens: New
Writing from Southern Africa* (2011) and was shortlisted for the PEN/Studzinski
Literary Award.

Printed in the United States of America

10 9 8 7 6 5 4 3 2 1

Library of Congress Cataloging-in-Publication Data
Names: Sacks, Michelle, 1980– author.
Title: Stone baby : stories / Michelle Sacks.
Description: Evanston, Illinois : Northwestern University Press, 2017.
Identifiers: LCCN 2017038004| ISBN 9780810136151 (pbk. : alk. paper) |
    ISBN 9780810136168 (e-book)
Classification: LCC PR9369.4.S235 S76 2017 | DDC 823.92—dc23
LC record available at https://lccn.loc.gov/2017038004

For my parents

Contents

KINGDOM

In the doorway of the bar, in his usual place, was Kingdom: tall, broad, full of fight and charm in equal doses and both proven to be fatal.

I am Kingdom, and this is my kingdom, he liked to say to the people who didn't already know it. But most of them did. They came to him for this or that—a score, a favor, a fuck. The girls knew where to find him, the German backpackers and Swedish students who wanted a taste of the dark side and some of them a little more. Plenty of them went home with his baby in their belly.

They touched his skin, the smoothness, the darkness; intoxicated with all that was new and exotic. What did he care? Two, twenty, didn't matter to him how many children there were when they were far away and likely never to be seen by him in the flesh. No one knew where he was from, nor what he'd done. His French was perfect, his English too, but any mother tongue he kept to himself. There were rumors, which he did nothing to encourage or deny; the scars on his face revealed something but not necessarily the truth, which is always open to speculation. Some of it he himself could barely recall. Was that life a nightmare or a dream, it was hard to say.

In any case, home now was here: this grubby patch of Long Street, this doorway of the Grind Bar, this cupboard-sized room upstairs with everything he owned in the world and everything that he would leave behind when he departed it. Bed, chair, pillow scavenged from the bar downstairs along with a plate, a mug, and a spoon. It was humble; it was all he needed. Better an inconspicuous hovel than something flash to draw attention to himself. Sameer—he called himself Sameer since the Imam at the Bo-Kaap mosque gave him a place to sleep and a hot meal once a week—was the closest thing to a friend that he had here, and even at that it's a push. Sameer came by some nights to talk, usually when he was high and full of ideas. His mother kicked him out of the house from time to time but Kingdom never offered him his room, only a few coins so he could buy something to eat when the hunger kicked in. Last winter he'd almost died in the doorway of the leather shop. The owner found him in the morning and called the cops to collect the body before he realized Sameer was not yet dead.

Jesus, he'd said to the cops, I guess I ought to have checked.

The cops shrugged and left; they didn't mind the callouts—it meant they could make their way back to the station nice and slow after a pie and a Coke.

Hasn't *meneer* got some work for me, Sameer asked through bleary eyes and that stinging pain in his head.

The man brought him tea and some biscuits and looked at him. Can you pick grapes? he said.

He sent Sameer to a wine farm in Robertson with a new pair of shoes and five hundred rand in his pocket.

White guilt, Sameer said, smiling his toothless smile for Kingdom before he left. It can move mountains.

He didn't last on the farm, got into too many fights, drank too much brandy, and couldn't figure out how to pick the grapes from the vines without bruising them. When he returned to Cape Town, he went straight home to his mother's, stole her new TV, and used the money to buy *tik* from his nephew. In town, he found Kingdom outside the bar, shook his hand, and offered him some of his stash.

Kingdom had lowered his voice, leaned in close, and whispered, bring me drugs again and I'll kill you.

He wasn't joking. He wasn't a man to joke.

Kingdom, he didn't care to get high, crazed, manic; there wasn't a rush in the world that he needed to try. Messed up too many, and ended always in the same pitiful way. He didn't mind selling. Rich kids could go ahead and kill themselves however they want, the poor too if it made them feel any better. But not for him, not for him. Besides, it wasn't obliteration he was after, it was sharpness, that acute sense of being alive and in the world, the hit to the gut that said, *yes, you are here.*

It's better you inspire fear in this life than love, his father told him when he was a boy, the only thing he said actually, or the only thing worth remembering.

And it was true. Kill. Cut. He'd do anything for money. The right people came his way, he'd get an envelope, a text, and it would be done. How did they find him? There was always a way. He didn't ask any questions because it was better not to know. He just did the job, washed his hands, pocketed the money. Some of them pleaded in those seconds when the reality of the situation became clear, tears streaking their faces and cheeks flush with blood and panic.

Why, they'd say, please, they'd cry, there must be another way.

But there wasn't.

Sorry, my friend, he'd say, it has nothing to do with me.

He always finished what he started. Kept it clean, kept it simple.

Bodies he knew where to drop. The city teemed with rotting flesh and the stink of something not right, but there were other smells that masked it: piss in the doorways, sex, broken bottles of booze; the uncollected bins the vagrants emptied onto the pavement in search of food. You could tell everything you needed to know about a country by the trash. First World trash, it was neat and orderly, organic muesli boxes folded like sheets to be dropped into the recycling bin, plastics squashed and sorted. Here, you found it all, the vestiges of a thousand shameful secrets; blood, needles, babies, everything disposable and disposed of. Every morning there was someone outside on the street with a bucket and a bottle of disinfectant, trying to wash away the night before, scrub, rinse, repeat, but you can't bleach it out, can you, the stink of a city, especially this one, infested with the poor, the vicious, the couldn't-give-a-fuck.

Hella, the Dutch girl, came by yesterday to tell him she was pregnant.

It's yours, she said.

He smiled, of course, baby, of course.

She wasn't upset, it was what she wanted. He'd lain with her till dawn in her narrow bed, holding her close, breathing in her smell. She was young, fierce, full of ideas. She wasn't beautiful, but she had something else. Men were mesmerized.

You out here saving African orphans or building houses for the poor? Those were Kingdom's first words to her and she had thrown her head back and laughed.

It's so obvious? She dropped her cigarette and stood on it with her sandal.

He'd nodded. Oh yes.

Her friends were inside the bar and she went to join them. Later, she was back outside, a little more liquor in her, a little more flirtatious. Kingdom watched, made her laugh, let himself imagine the body beneath her dress. He could see how she looked at him, the longing. He turned it up, laid it on thick. He could do that, in a heartbeat, make himself into whatever cliché they wanted.

Her friends came outside, ready to leave. It was after four A.M., things were winding down, people pouring out of the bars and making their way to their cars or to the boerewors vendors. She looked at him and hesitated, and so he winked and said what she needed to hear.

Night's too young to go home, baby.

Her friends were Dutch too, but there was one who was a local. You could always tell them apart. She looked wide-eyed at the scene, whispered something to Hella, and tried to steer her away.

It's okay, Kingdom smiled, she's safe with me.

The girl glared at him, threw up her hands. It's your life, she said to Hella.

They took a taxi back to the apartment Hella was renting, a nice block in Sea Point. The doorman looked momentarily panicked at the sight of Kingdom's hand on her back, but Hella said brightly, it's okay Eric, he's just here to fuck me.

In the bed he turned her over onto her stomach and pinned her down with the weight of his body against hers.

You have a condom, he said.

No, she lied. Do it anyway.

He pushed into her, wet and warm; she moaned and moved her hips back against him. You sure? he asked, and she said yes, yes, and so he finished.

You want a souvenir, he laughed.

She lay beside him, and he traced her breasts with a finger. It still intrigued him, the whiteness of white flesh, the shock of it against his own skin. She was here for a semester of her Ph.D.; anthropology, she said, because people fascinated her. She wanted him to talk, to tell her about the scars and the accent and where he'd come from. He shook his head, found his jeans. It's not a good bedtime story, he said.

On his way out, he flashed Eric a smile.

Most days Kingdom slept, curled up like a baby on the too-soft mattress in his room. It was nights he was awake and on the prowl, a lion sussing out what he'll eat next, watching, waiting. Days he couldn't sleep for too much noise or the restlessness that came from time to time, he sat in the café on the corner and observed people come and go. Tourists with their cameras poised, sneaking shots of people as they went about their day, locals too, some working, some hoping to work. The rainbow nation, he thought, but there was no pot of gold anywhere here. Just this, the daily slog, the fight for life. The city was the best education he'd ever had. Watch long enough and you'd figure it all out. The nuances of daily life, the seekers, the searchers, the swindlers. Who's looking for what and why, because everyone wanted something. He heard of places like New York and Paris, the cities that never slept, but right here was action enough, a constant pageant of disparate faces from here, there, who knows where. All of them, and him. Kingdom, Kingdom.

Today was one of the restless days, mind racing, a hum in his veins, but he didn't have the time to watch the hours pass from the comfort of his usual spot. There was a job, someone to meet, money to be made. He splashed his face with water, put on a fresh shirt laundered for him by Mandy, the waitress at the corner café who had a washing machine and liked to exchange clean clothes for a small bag of weed from time to time. On the way out, Kingdom bumped into Sameer. He shook his hand and smelled of something strong from the night before or maybe even this morning. His eyes were red and there was dried blood around the corners of his mouth.

What happened? Kingdom asked.

My mother, Sameer said.

You stealing from her again?

Sameer laughed, mouth mostly empty of teeth. The front ones were taken in some kind of gang initiation, the rest were casualties of *tik* and fists.

Nah, my brother, Sameer said, only borrowing, only borrowing.

She'll kill you one day, Kingdom said, but Sameer was off his head, good for nothing and least of all sense. He'd be dead soon for sure, looked near death most days, and if the drugs didn't get him the dealers would. Still, Kingdom felt nothing, nothing to feel. So what if Sameer got a brick in the face from his own mother. Wouldn't be the first or the last. Keep it light, keep it light. Fewer things in his life, fewer things to lose, to grieve, to long for. That was survival: knowing it could all be lost, preparing for the inevitability.

Street kids he passed were begging for money, sizing up handbags clutched tight to their owners' sides because no one here was stupid anymore. Even the tourists had stopped wearing their cameras round their necks. They were warned before they set foot on the plane. Africa, Africa, the same rules don't apply. As he walked by, the kids turned to look at him but they didn't ask for money, they knew he wouldn't give any. Some of them called out to him, Kingdom, Kingdom; they wanted to be like him or thought they did. Dumb kids without a chance in hell, born on the streets, streets till they die. Winter mornings you'd see some of them frozen stiff, wrapped in cardboard boxes to stay warm but hearts given out all the same. Once, Kingdom had walked by a body laid out by the cops, the face covered with a sheet of Christmas wrapping paper from inside the stationery store because there was nothing else on hand. The boy must have been eight, maybe ten, but the shoes sticking out belonged to an adult. People were gathered, a woman wiped a tear with the back of her hand. Kingdom didn't linger. Under the right circumstances, death could be as kind as it could be cruel and certainly around these parts. Everybody had a story, a tragedy wrapped in a heartache. Kingdom had heard it all, seen with his own eyes the townships and the streets and the faces of people alive but dead inside, enough wretchedness to rip you in two but still he'd shrug it off, walk away, because there was no understanding it or fixing it, only surviving it.

The man he was due to meet got hold of him through a man who knew a man. The trail could never lead to him, too tangled, too many nameless names. Suited him, he wanted no trouble, no upsets. You could do that here, stay anonymous, undocumented. There were millions just like him, born one man and reborn another as soon as they crossed the border. Some of them went to the trouble of going to Home Affairs, getting a photograph taken, signing up for an official ID book. Name? they'd ask at the counter, and you could offer up whatever you wanted. James, Jesus, Michael Fucking Jordan. Birth certificate, driver's license, there wasn't anything you couldn't get your hands on if you needed it. Kingdom, he'd chosen to stay under the radar, no fingerprints, no name in a computer. Just him, loose like water, moving in and out as he pleased. No one demanded much more from him, and if they did, he wasn't interested. His money he kept in his room, fat rolls stashed into books he'd cut the pages out of. He saw that in a movie once, *The Shawshank Redemption* it was, thought it was the cleverest thing he'd ever seen and decided to do the same. If he ever needed to leave in a hurry, all he'd need to take along were his books and his name.

The man said noon outside the church, but he was nowhere and Kingdom had to wait. The outer wall of the church had been fitted with barbed wire, ready to cut, ready to draw blood from trespassers. This was the world, this was how it had to be. The sun was shining and everyone was spilled out onto the streets. It was the time of year for tourists and they were everywhere, being shown beaded animals and chickens made from trash bags. Six vendors to a tourist and all of them with a story and the hope of a sale.

Please Ma, he overheard, just buy one so I can get some food for my wife.

The woman fell for it, fished in her moonbag for money, and while doing so revealed how much there was in her wad of notes. Fifty rand she peeled off for him in exchange for a beaded green giraffe. The man was crushed she didn't take more, it wouldn't put a dent in her traveler's checks to take the lot.

Only one? he said. What about some presents for your friends?

She laughed and shook her head, no, not today.

He moved quickly onto the next person without saying goodbye or showing her the gratitude that usually won the tourists over. Zimbabwean, maybe Congolese, Kingdom couldn't place where he was from but like him it wasn't here. The locals hated them all, no matter where they came from. You steal our jobs, they said, but how could they?

There weren't any to take. They made their own jobs, sold bananas at the bus stop and ice lollies at the soccer games. Slow, painstaking savings, every penny paving the way for the next generation to have it a little better. The locals Kingdom knew felt entitled, wanted it handed out and not earned.

The tension was heavy, sometimes fatal. SAY NO TO XENOPHOBIA! The posters lined the streets when the violence flared up, usually every few months. But many of the ones looting the foreign-owned *spazas* or setting fire to whichever unfortunate they managed to corner could barely read. All they had was their hate, the terror that they would find themselves with even less. And yet, the rest of the continent kept pouring in, sure of nothing but the fact that this pitiful life, this half-life with no jobs, no home, no money, would still be better than before, better than the life they left behind in whatever godforsaken place they'd come from.

The locals didn't realize how good they had it, even the ones who had it bad. War, torture, one massacre after the next; how many limbs he'd seen cut from living flesh like a branch off a tree. You want suffering, you have to go further north than this piece of paradise. When Kingdom remembered—correction, when he allowed himself to remember—there was still one thing that could send a pain to his heart that cut him like a knife, one face, one name, one monumental failure. Dembe. She might be alive, but mostly it was easier imagining her dead, more clear-cut. When the thoughts of his baby sister came, he pinched himself on the soft skin between his thumb and forefinger till the pain was stronger than the memory.

When he'd first arrived in South Africa, young and feeling lucky, he saw soon enough how things worked, how it was for people like him, the broken and the exiled. Not for him, though, not for him. He was young but had no fear; when all that's good is already gone, it makes it easier. He made friends, the right ones, always willing to do what nobody else would. They liked him, not the locals of course, but the others like him. Nigerians, Somalis, Kenyans. The ones with an ear to the ground and a nose for making money. It was them who gave him his name, more than his name, but it was the name he'd never forget, the thing he'd take with him wherever came next. It was a joke, for them, bestowed on a boy who was never a child, but he took it, held it close because it was his and from them he learned the tricks of survival. Who to trust, who to fear. All of them were long gone, dead from disease or discord or moved onto Joburg for the promise of something more. They weren't friends, but teachers. He owed them his thanks and gave it freely because it was only for them that he had it so good. Had what he needed, took what he could get. Knew he couldn't ask for more, all things considered, but that was just fine. It was enough.

Finally, the man with the red cap arrived, nodded his head in silent greeting. He walked past, took Kingdom's hand to shake it, and in the exchange a note found its way into his fingers. Always the same, even though there weren't nearly enough police around to be watching the goings-on of a few petty thugs anyway. Besides, the dead men dead from Kingdom's hand, well, they were not the ones who mattered. Lowlifes, cheats, the dregs that needed to be taken off the streets one way or the other. It was nothing to him. One less here was always one more somewhere else. He strolled back through the company gardens, bought a bag of peanuts from the woman who sat at the entrance every day come rain or shine, and threw most of them to the squirrels. There was a man nearby talking loudly into his phone.

Yes, he said, I also want to believe we can do this amicably, but it seems like you're out to fuck me over at every turn. He hurled the phone into the bushes and then went to retrieve it, getting mud on his tan leather shoes.

Never marry a cunt, he said to Kingdom.

At the McDonald's on Kloof Street, Kingdom ordered a burger and fries, drenched both in mustard, and devoured it all in a few bites. He wiped his hands on his jeans and put the little plastic tray on the trolley. A child was crying, her mother crouched over her showing her the toy that had come in the Happy Meal. Her hand-bag was on the floor next to her, unzipped and with her leather wallet on full display. There was a time he might have taken it, but not these days.

Watch your bag, he said.

As he left he knew she'd be rifling through her wallet, certain he'd already cleared it out. Outside the Grind Bar were the usual loiterers and layabouts, the day crowd who were there only for lack of a better option. Friedl, the owner, called him over.

Got some more books for you, he said.

His wife ran a charity shop, skimmed off the copies of donated books already in stock and boxed them up for Kingdom.

Kingdom took the books, thanked Friedl, and joined him for a pot of tea. Friedl has been sober ten years, bought the bar the same day he quit drinking. Need the discipline, he explained. Upstairs, Kingdom kicked off his shoes, wet his face at the little basin, and lay down on the never-made bed. He took the note from his pocket, unfolded it. It was typed, just a name, an address. All he needed. The money would come later, different hat, different man underneath, a wholly efficient system. Kingdom shut his eyes, tried to sleep. He thought of Hella, his baby inside her. She'd gone to Namibia after their night together, been away just long enough to return with a slight bump.

Look, she'd said, feel it.

He refused, she insisted. Eventually, he put his hand there, felt her belly hard beneath it, filling up from the inside.

It's okay, she said, I know the deal. I just wanted to show you.

She was going surfing in Indonesia and then back home, to Antwerp or Amsterdam or wherever it was that she lived. He would never see her again, never meet the child, who would likely come out just brown enough to give away its father's identity. Who knows what Hella would tell it, what story she'd make up. Kingdom put it out of his mind. Not his problem, not his life.

The noise downstairs from the street was a distant buzz, the ticking over of time below. He breathed deep and sleep came, the briefest respite. He didn't dream anymore, too long blocking it out and it stopped altogether. There was only darkness now, and stillness.

Hours later, it was dark and cool. The blind on his window clinked against the frame and Kingdom woke, rubbing his eyes. He took his time, ambled downstairs, no rush, no rush. Friedl didn't employ him so much as expect him. He came and went, took a cut, broke up a few fights, and saw fit to join others. Mostly, it was a place to be each night, a place where he could be found. Up the street, down the street, everyone could point you in the direction of Kingdom. The night started slow, too early in the week for much to happen. There were regulars who came by, greeted him by name, bumped fists with him to show their friends just how street they could be. Kingdom indulged some of them, others he withered with a look. It was power, might as well enjoy it, might as well play along.

Midnight and it was just a handful still inside, drinking, smoking in the courtyard, trying to cop a feel. He got a Coke from the barman, sat on the chair in the doorway, and let the ice melt into his cheek. A girl stumbled in, skirt up to her underwear and make-up smudged. She was alone and trouble, but it was nothing to do with him. He watched a kid climb into a sports car parked across the street. Soon as the car guard came running for his tip, the kid pulled away. The car guard shook his head, cursed in French. Kingdom called something to him that made both men laugh. More time passed. The drunk girl emerged, this time on the arm of a boy looking like the cat who got the cream. Didn't even have to woo her. Maybe she'd pass out before, maybe not. A guy with a beard came over to tell him his phone had been stolen.

Maybe it fell out of your pocket, Kingdom said.

The guy said, no, it was stolen, right off the bar.

Kingdom shrugged. Sorry friend, can't help you.

The guy started getting stroppy, Kingdom half rose from his stool, just enough to show how much of him there was to mess with. Okay, okay, the guy backed up, crossed the street, disappeared into a different bar. All the comings and goings, they were like tides that washed up some things and swept others off to God knows where. Ebb and flow, ebb and flow; the story of the universe.

Just before closing time, the man came along, handed over a Kentucky Fried Chicken bag that was one part wings, one part cash. He said, tonight, and Kingdom nodded. He waited for Friedl to lock up, said good night, and then took the bag and headed upstairs. He ate the wings, which were spicy and crisp, chewed the bones and gristle and licked the grease off his fingers. The money he counted, then rolled. Into the book it went, the worn copy of *Moby-Dick* that Friedl's wife had given him some months back along with a Bible.

Wasn't sure if you preferred whales or God, she'd said.

It was late but he was not tired, he was buzzing. Business to take care of. Partly it was the adrenaline, partly the feeling that it could always be his last. He checked the address, which was close enough to walk. He waited an hour longer for the street to clear out and then headed off, gun cocked, knife ready. In and out, no questions, no room to doubt. Outside the property, he was a little surprised. Nice neighborhood, warning sign from an alarm company. This wasn't what he was used to, but the man who knew the man who knew the man wouldn't have made any mistakes. The street was deserted, no dogs, no guards, nobody but himself and the steady thrum of his heart in his chest. One last time he checked around to see if he was alone and then he was in—over the wall, into the garden. He could smell roses and jasmine. He checked his watch, waited five minutes to see if he had triggered any alarm but he appeared to be in the clear. He walked around the house, found a side door. It was an old house, one of the original Victorians. Sturdy but no fortress, which was just his luck. With the screwdriver from his pocket he took the handle off the door, screw by screw, working by touch until he was holding it in his hands. The lock he just had to push back with a finger and he was in, treading quietly, light like a mouse in the house. The wooden floors creaked as he walked, he tried to stay on the rugs, working his way to the bedroom. He put his head into a room but no one was inside; another room, same story. Finally, he poked his head into a doorway and could make out the shape of a bed. He inched into the room with just a little trepidation, steady, steady.

I didn't think you would make it, said a voice.

Kingdom froze; panic worked its way right down to his toes. Stomach lurching, sweat sticky on the back of his neck, he asked, you have a gun?

The voice, a woman's, laughed. No. But you do, I hope.

Kingdom, confused, disoriented in the dark, took the gun from his belt, cocked it, pointed it at the voice. What the fuck's going on? he said.

There was silence, nothing but the tension thick and loud in the air. Suspense. Dread. Everything unknown in the darkness.

Oh, I'm sorry, the voice said, calm and cool. I thought you knew.

Knew what? Kingdom shouted. You want to play games, find someone else. He was enraged to be caught off guard, stumbling in the dark like an amateur.

But you are here . . . to do a job, shall we say? the voice said.

Yes, a job, he replied.

Good, she said, that is good. I am your job.

The gun itched in his hands, Kingdom stood on one leg and then the other. Lady, you're crazy in the head. I don't know what you're talking about.

He was pissed as hell, blood boiling.

If you leave without doing the job you don't get paid, the voice said. I should think this is a normal condition in your line of work.

Kingdom sank to his haunches, put his head in his hands, and didn't know whether to laugh, cry, or shoot.

The voice continued. I am the one who hired you. Your client, as it were.

You're the boss? he said. Okay. Okay. So what is it you are hiring me for?

I think you already know.

Suddenly, Kingdom became aware of movement in the room, not from the direction of the voice but from somewhere else.

My husband, the voice said. He takes a sleeping pill every night, he won't wake.

Kingdom, still reeling, tried to keep calm, tried to piece together the situation at hand.

The woman continued, even and unemotional as the words hung in the air, heavy in the dark but not yet sinking in.

It is my husband you are here for, she said. He is the man you are being paid to . . . to terminate.

Kingdom was silent.

Is that a good way of putting it? the woman said.

Fine, Kingdom said. Let me do what you're paying me for and get the fuck out of here.

You don't even ask why, she said.

I don't care, Kingdom replied.

How is that possible? she asked, for the first time with less certainty in her voice.

He beats you, rapes you, cheats on you, Kingdom replied. None of it is anything to do with me. Even if you just want his money, nice and cold, it means nothing to me. Your business is your business, your life is your life.

There was silence, a soft rustling of the sheets.

He's a good man. The best kind, in fact, she said.

Still you want him gone.

He's sick, she said.

In sickness and in health—you didn't make a promise? Kingdom sneered.

He didn't want to be here, discussing this with a woman who was paying him to take someone out.

He'll get too sick. He doesn't want that, she said.

He wants a bullet in his brain?

It's more dignified, she said. Death, rather than illness. I would expect him to do the same for me actually. We discussed it. We made a pact. It's a lot less cruel than it sounds.

Like I said, Kingdom replied, makes no difference to me. But if you have it all worked out, why do you need me?

Well, the woman said, and he could hear from her voice that she was neither young nor unafraid. If I do the job, there is a far greater chance of me being punished than if you do it.

She laughed, nervous, brittle like glass. Such is our justice system, she said. Kingdom smirked too, because it was funny and also strange to be having this conversation about justice, with a gun in one hand and a body below it waiting to be the target.

He has Alzheimer's, she said. He's going to forget his own name soon. He's already forgotten mine. There's worse to come, only worse, because it doesn't get better. The world just gets increasingly alien. We become strangers. The people who know him best, who love him most in the world. We become unknown to him, and him to us.

Kingdom waited, said nothing because already he'd said too much. He knew about Alzheimer's, old-timer's disease. Forgetting your name, forgetting to eat and where to piss and how to pull a shirt over your head. In fairness, it was one of the better reasons to want to be dead.

I'm going to kiss him, the woman said, and then I want you to do it. Quickly. Yes?

I can't see properly, Kingdom said. You need to put a light on.

There was a pause, she was thinking; weighing up the options.

But then I'll know your face, she said.

Kingdom laughed, nervous or amused it was hard to know. Then maybe I'll have to kill you too, he said.

There was a pause and then a light went on, soft light from a side lamp with a heavy shade. His eyes took in the room, plush and nicely furnished, paintings on the walls, family photographs in silver frames beside the bed. A son, a daughter. The woman was lying in the bed atop the covers, beside the man she had hired a stranger to kill. The man didn't look older than sixty, he didn't look sick or frail, just like a man who was sleeping. The woman took a hand to his cheek and stroked it with such aching tenderness that Kingdom wanted to look away. She kissed him, on the lips, on the cheek, on each of his firmly shut eyelids. Her act of love. Her act of mercy. She did not look at Kingdom as she turned her head away from her husband.

Do it, she said.

Kingdom pointed, no flinching, no thinking. He fired the gun. One, two, the crack of gunpowder and the shock of flesh. The man did not even cry out before he went still, dead in the bed that was now a coffin. Kingdom, like always, felt nothing, just business, just another job, but as he turned to the woman he saw something he did not anticipate. A gun in her own hands, pointed at him, sharp and steady like an arrow.

I'm sorry, she said, but it is always best without loose ends. And you are an intruder, after all.

Before he had time to think, to shoot, the gun fired, the bullets hit—one, two, three, he stopped counting at four—and the pain was too great and the blood poured too fast and he dropped to the floor, first to his knees and then out flat, splayed like a hide and almost as dead. The woman he could hear on the phone, crying, feigning distress. Yes, officer, she was saying, my husband's been shot.

She was hysterical, very convincing, but he lost interest in the conversation because he was leaking onto the carpet one globule of life at a time.

No, no, he thought and forced what was left of his brain to think of a place, and a face, that place and that face, *home, Dembe*, and he imagined that he was not here, bleeding out the last of life, but there, starting at the very beginning. The blood seeped, the noises around him ceased to be audible.

As his gaze followed the pool of blood spreading beneath him and his breath became shorter and scarcer and soon almost not-there-at-all, he summoned, with everything he had left, a smile to his lips; for irony, for life, for that he lived at all.

I am Kingdom, he thought, and this is my kingdom.

MOCKINGBIRD

How do you come to be here? This is the question, and not for the first time. It's a woman, maybe his age, carrying a little too much around the middle, skin tanned and leathery and slicked with lotion to draw in more sun. She's with her daughter, the two of them have come in for lunch.

Is it spicy? the mother asked, I like a little kick but not so hot that it ruins my mascara. No, he says, it's not too spicy, just the right amount.

He hears himself describing green curries to tourists and wants to laugh or cry or run into traffic. But no, she's asked the question now and he needs to answer. Smile, laugh, *oh you know, it's a long story*. Actually they usually just want to clarify that he's not some kind of a pedophile. Sometimes he even says it. *Don't worry, I'm not here because of the lenient child sex laws.* Badabing badabang! Tricky one to judge, though, because that kind of response can go horribly wrong, especially coming from a pasty Westerner of his age. This one's a talker. Long story doesn't put her off. She may even be flirting with him, right in front of her daughter. In fact, the daughter is watching her, watching him, smiling, egging her mother on. Maybe she's newly divorced. Newly widowed. The daughter turns to her phone while the mother looks at him expectantly.

Love, she says, or money? I mean, that's usually the only two plausible reasons to leave one place for another, isn't it?

Sure, he nods, sure. In that case, love, he says. I'm here for love.

When he brings the food there's not much more chitchat, they've figured out he's a dismal prospect.

You call this not spicy, the mother says, dabbing at her eyes. Look at this, look at my face.

Ah sure, he says, it's a lovely face, spice or no spice.

He's said the right thing, they tip well when they leave. Angie, who owns the place, gives him a wink.

Harry baby, she says, you born for this.

Harry does a little bow, a tip of the imaginary hat. Gift of the gab, baby, he says, knowing she'll use it later.

She's been collecting his phrases, his Irishisms, trying to improve her English. The words always come out wrong when she says them but he doesn't have the heart to tell her. She's a good woman. Or a good man, if you look at it that way, which he's stopped doing. Took him in like a broken-winged bird, held his hand as he wept at her bar the first night he was here, told him a job and a room were his if he wanted them; helped him translate documents and call up reporters. In return she asked for nothing, not one thing. Shocks Harry, the setup he has here, the transition from then to now. One life one minute and another the next, literally worlds apart but normal has a funny way of creeping up on you, and this now, this is the norm.

He grabs a sip of water from his bottle behind the bar. The heat he can't get used to, imagines he never will. Back in the day, him and the lads went down to the south of Spain twice a year, stayed at Mick's villa in Marbella and spent their days drinking cheap beer and soaking up as much sun as they could bear.

Isn't this the life? they'd say. Sun, sea, ten euro steaks.

Nights they'd go to the Irish pub, Mallone's or Grady O's, eat dinner, listen to the live bands, deconstruct the last football game they'd watched, or reminisce about the previous year's trip to Spain. They walked back to the house in the warm night air, breathed in the smell of the sea, and reckoned there was no more they could ask of their time on earth. They made noises always about moving somewhere warm, retiring anywhere but Ireland with its dismal climate and poor service. Still, not one of them could ever do it, actually leave. They blamed the wives or the kids or the economy, though in truth they never proposed it at all and they all knew why.

You could say Harry's adjusted well. This job, a place to stay, a daily routine that helps him stay marginally sane. In the beginning Mick Skyped him from the car.

Jaysus, I admire you, Harry, he'd said. What you've gone and done. Don't think I could do it.

Mick, Harry said, what other choice do I have?

But of course he had a choice—look at Helen, back in Dalkey, life just as before. Tennis on Wednesdays, morning walks with the girls down to the harbor, Sunday service at St. Patrick's. Oh, we're grand, she'd be saying, we're all grand. Everyone would know, because of course they'd have seen the news, read the papers, but still they'd smile and nod and go back to the weather.

It wasn't that Helen didn't feel guilt over Lissa. She just refused to feel responsible. Whereas Harry, well. Look at him. Man of sixty, waiting tables in The Happy Bar & Food in Kuta, sweating from every pore, hemorrhaging away his life savings on lawyers despite their own advice that he stop. All of it for Lissa. All of it in the vain hope that if he only stays close and keeps hoping, things might just change.

Logically, he knows, chances are nil. But Lissa and logic have never gone hand in hand. Lissa. His baby girl. Beautiful and bright, whole world at her feet. He saw her last week and wept right in front of her, broke down and could do nothing to stop his face from crumpling and his body from shaking with tears and rage.

Dad, she said, please stop.

He couldn't touch her hand, couldn't kiss her, one on each cheek and one on the tip of her nose like he used to do when she was six; couldn't say, it's alright pet, everything will be okay because it wasn't and wouldn't be ever again.

Fifteen years, best—absolutely best-case scenario—is what the lawyers were working toward but the likelihood was longer. They don't like to show leniency on foreigners, the lawyer said. Only they believe it makes them look like they're kowtowing to Western influence, politics and money and such. His name was Kowalski, a hard as nails Pole whose mother and aunt drove three hours from Poland into Germany each day to clean houses and put the children through school. Harry had found him in London, cashed in his pension and paid him in advance for his services. Kowalski explained the gravity of the situation several times, nice and slow like he was talking to a child.

Please, Mr. Hickey, you need to keep your expectations in check. A case like this . . .

A case like this was Lissa, half a kilo of heroin packed into a fake plaster cast on her arm and a boyfriend who sold her out in exchange for a better sentence. Case like this was, she was fucked.

When Lissa had bought the plane ticket and told them she was off for a year, Helen was pleased.

It would be good for her, she said. Maybe she'll finally learn about taking responsibility. Harry wasn't sure, something didn't feel right.

Sweet Jesus, Harry, Helen said, that child's been indulged long enough.

She didn't have to add *by you*, because Harry knew that's what she thought anyway. He was happy to admit it too, that she'd had him wrapped around her finger since the day she was born. Daddy's girl. Someone would make the remark and inside he'd want to burst with happiness. He can see the early years like a movie in his head, grainy and too bright. Helen presenting him with a little stick that said YES, the first ultrasound where they listened to the urgent pounding of her grain-sized heart, Helen cupping her belly the way all pregnant women do, as though trying to stop the child from falling through to the ground. The smell of the delivery room cigars and the first terrifying bath he gave her in the kitchen sink when Helen was struck down with the flu, the incessant screeching from the crib and then the unforgettable magic of the first gummy smile she gave him. The memories came in a rush when he let them, but the later ones were always a little less rosy.

He would like to blame the school, the friends she made, that wretched Conor, who ruined it all. He does, he blames everyone and everything, but he blames himself more. She's no angel, Harry, Helen likes to remind him, our daughter was instrumental in carving out this fate for herself.

Helen, when the fuck, he wonders, did she get so hard, so detached? Years now she's spoken of Lissa like she's already long departed. Our daughter was. Lissa used to be. Past tense, everything already behind them.

We have to move forward, she said, make lives for ourselves that aren't dictated to by Lissa and her dramas.

She was right, most probably, but he couldn't reconcile the idea of having a daughter with the idea of cutting her off. It wasn't the reason for the divorce but it didn't help things either. Helen might have stayed if she'd felt less alone in the marriage, less sacrificed in the name of the errant child.

When he'd gotten the call he'd packed his bag in ten minutes flat: a few shirts, deodorant, heart pills. He booked a one-way flight, said, I'm not coming back without her, kissed his mother good-bye, and stepped into a cab. He arrived in Jakarta, spent some nights there making calls, trying to plead Lissa's case to anyone he could find. The heat, the humidity, the stench, and the never-ending swarm of people. Hell, he thought, this is surely what it's like in hell. Nothing was familiar, nothing was like anywhere he'd been or seen. Noise, garbage, collapse. A city for the end of the world. He hated the food, too spicy, too much heat, no sense of hygiene. He walked through the markets, watched women carrying dripping meat through the streets with their bare hands. His stomach felt like it was rotting from the inside, the cramps hard like a fist clenched over his intestines, the toilet bowl every morning a massacre. In his hotel room the air-conditioning dripped water through the night onto the carpet while the street below thrummed with noise and catastrophe.

You're not doing anyone any good over there, Helen said when he called to update her. She won't even thank you for it, you know.

She could be cold like ice, Helen, but seldom wrong. When he got to Kuta and saw Lissa for the first time she hardly registered when he told her he wasn't just visiting.

I'll be here, he said, whatever it takes, however long. I'm not leaving without you.

She looked at him, face blank, eyes unblinking, skin pale and full of blotches like she'd been picking at it. She seemed very thin but her belly was bloated—for a horrifying second he thought she might be pregnant too and dared to ask.

What are you like, Dad, she said. I just haven't had a shit in two weeks.

She was in Kerobokan Prison, one of the worst. Harry had never set foot in a prison before, let alone something like this. Reeking, fetid, a babel of voices and disease hanging in the air. How will she survive this, Harry thought, and a voice in his head replied, *maybe she won't.*

You want to trace it back, find the root of the problem: X marks the spot. Too much TV or not enough hugs or a working mother. None of it matters, though, because none of it can be undone.

It wasn't my fault, Dad, she said, not for the first time.

And of course he'll believe her, to his dying day, just like he believed her when she was fourteen and got caught smoking behind the tennis courts at school and then when she was fifteen and got sent to St. James to have her stomach pumped from alcohol poisoning and then when she was eighteen and the Garda came to the door to say she'd been arrested for selling ecstasy inside the ladies' toilet at some club. He'd believed her when she said it was Conor Walsh who put the first line of cocaine in front of her and he believed her when she sat sobbing in a heap on his doorstep telling him she needed twenty thousand euros to pay a dealer Walsh had screwed over and he believed her ten times over when she looked at him with those eyes that were his eyes and promised she was going to get her life together if only he could help her out one last time.

Daddy. That was all she's ever had to say.

It's paradise, Kuta. He can see it the way other people see it. The stretch of beach, the color of the sea, the smiles the locals flash before they try to sell you something. There are foreigners who stay for months; some never leave. Some days, he even heads down to the beach himself, takes an hour to float in the warmth of the ocean, not quite above or below the surface, just suspended there in the water like a pause.

He watches families on vacation, scrutinizes their interactions. How are they doing it, what measures are they putting in place now to keep their children out of harm's way in the future. Angie's cousin visits the restaurant with her baby, a fat-cheeked six-month-old who slays Harry every time she smiles at him. The cousin gives the child to Harry to hold and he tries always to refuse. Look at me, he wants to scream, look at what a mess I made before.

The things that bothered him here in the beginning don't even register now. Cold bucket showers, food that shreds his insides, bugs crawling on the pillow or burrowing into his flesh. Sunburn. Sweat stains that won't wash out. The almost constant threat of flooding during monsoon season or the tsunamis that seem to be becoming a regular event. Last month, half of South Kuta was washed away. Busloads of islanders shipped out clutching as many suitcases as they could carry, doomed travelers on the worst trip of their lives. Harry watches the news with his heart in his throat, chaos and despair unrelenting. Still, nothing is worse for him than it is for Lissa. Nothing he suffers is greater than her suffering. He welcomes it actually, every discomfort, everything that in another life would have made him boil over. They used to go camping in France over the summer, pack up the station wagon, load up Lissa and all her toys. She loved the ferry, driving the car onto the water and sailing over to Calais. Half the neighbors would be there too, heading off for some budget sun in the days before twenty euro flights to the Canaries. In France, Helen spent the time reading on the fold-up chair, Lissa played games with the other kids or swam in the lakes, and Harry counted the days till they could pack up and go home.

He hated the campsites, the trickling showers, the inane chitchat with the other dads, the baguette every morning for breakfast. He missed the TV and Friday nights with the lads, felt his back ache from the blow-up mattress, and fumbled along in rusty high school French every time he needed to ask for the bill. Five long weeks they camped each summer, and every year Harry suffered in silence, feeling ennobled by his sacrifice. He looks back now and sees that those were the best years of his life.

I love you. I'm waiting for you. Daddy's here. He says the same words every day, to Lissa, to himself. He wants to believe she knows it, feels it. He wants to believe it makes a difference despite all evidence to the contrary. Once a week he sees her, reports back. Progress is being made, he lies.

She looks worse every time. Hair falling out, skin a mess. She tells him she's been befriended by an Australian girl, a lifer. He tries to think what that means. From his bedroom window he hears the Imam's calls to prayer. He never knew a single Muslim in Dublin, only saw them with their headscarves from time to time on the train. He knows they have faith, strict rules they live by. He hopes this will count in Lissa's favor in prison. He always makes sure to smile at the guards, says please and thank you as though they were hotel staff showing him the pool cabanas. They don't smile back, don't pity him or his child because why would they. All that privilege, all that education and opportunity, and this is the best she can do with her life. They're scornful, is what they are.

Angie, dressed in another skintight dress to show off her new tits, sashays over to Harry, fan in hand to keep her makeup from melting.

You hear news today? she asks.

Yes, he says, today's the day.

There's a young couple outside, reading the menu. They kick off their shoes and come inside. They look surprised when Harry walks over to take their order, probably thought he was a customer. They order Bintangs and he carries them to the table, ice-cold from the fridge. He pours the drinks, feels a lump grow thick in his throat.

Kids, maybe midtwenties, first big trip he'd guess because they've got every bit of gear imaginable. Angie comes over to their table, asks as she always does where they're from. Iceland, they say, and she runs to stick a pin in the world map that covers the wall behind the bar. Harry brings them their food, tries not to watch them as they eat. So young, all of life ahead of them. The girl reads from the guidebook and marks things with a pen. He wonders if they call home enough.

When the lunch crowd has emptied out it's just him and Angie and a Dutch girl sitting in the corner with a sketchbook. She's a few months' pregnant by the looks of it, belly bare over a sarong tied at her waist. Harry didn't see a ring when he served her, no boyfriend or husband has come to join her at the table. Harry can't get over it, even now. The kids today. The things they get away with. He and Angie sit by the fan while she reapplies foundation in her bedazzled pocket mirror. He gives a little wolf whistle, makes her smile. It's refreshing for her, attention from a man who doesn't care to see what's between her legs. She gives Harry's cheek a little peck and he returns it with a wink. He owes her. He may even love her.

I'm, what you say, myself-made woman? she told him the night they met.
Self-made, Harry said.
Yeah, she nodded, self-made, because I make myself.
Into a woman? Harry asked.
Into a business! she'd replied.
On her eleventh birthday, her parents told her she should be a woman instead of a man. There was no gender confusion, it was about cold hard cash.
Here, men could make money with drugs or crime, women with their bodies. Her parents had done the math and decided for her. Harry looked at her with a mix of awe and horror. The tits, the affected speech, the swinging hips, all of it just for money.
He shook his head, Jesus, Mary, and Joseph, he said, how can you still keep a smile on your face?

Angie danced her hands in the air. Life sometimes is good, sometimes is bad. But always it is life. And so we have reason to smile.

She offered him a blow job then and he politely declined.

Better, she said. We become best friends instead.

Harry imagined it sometimes, what it must look like from the outside, him and Angie, heads bent together, chatting for hours like old friends. Mick, he'd have a field day, Neil and Kev too. *What in the bejesus are you doing over there with a trannie?*

In Dublin he'd cross the street if he saw two men hand in hand, just because. His own nephew Robbie, whatever he was it was far from normal. But here, what does he care. Angie's family.

The phone rings and Angie swings round the bar to answer it.

For you, she says, and his heart races.

He takes a breath, takes the phone. This is it.

Harry, says the voice, it's Kowalski. How's the line, can you hear me?

He's back in London, left as soon as he could. His last words to Harry as they shook hands: Go home. Harry knew he meant well.

I can hear, Harry says into the phone. He clutches his free hand around the handle of a knife lying on the counter. *I love you. I'm waiting for you. Daddy's here.* Kowalski coughs and he knows what's coming next.

News isn't good, Harry, he says, I'm so sorry.

The repatriation application's been denied. Lissa's staying, which means he's staying. Just like that, his fate and hers, wrapped up together in a single phone call that determines the next two decades of their lives.

Harry? Kowalski says. We really did our best.

Harry puts the phone down, keeps his grip on the knife. Angie, reading his face, pours a double whiskey and sets it down in front of him.

Bottoms up, she says, and he drinks.

The burn is good, but not good enough. He takes the bottle and pours another. For the first time in months, maybe ever, he's mad at Lissa. Burning mad.

A kid walks in, beard growing down his neck, hair in a ponytail, shorts stiff with dirt.

I got it, Angie says, but Harry shakes his head.

I need distracting, he says.

He goes over to the table to take the order. The kid's South African or maybe Aussie, he can't much tell them apart. He picks at the mosquito bites on his arm and flicks the scabs onto the ground. When the food's ready, Harry takes it over, lays it down.

Your *nasi goreng*, he says.

Cheers, the kid replies, smiling bright. Hey man, he leans in, you know somewhere I can score a little something around here?

He thinks Harry's a hippie, a junkie like him, one of those tourists who arrive and never leave because growing old stoned and in the sun is a far better option than anything back at home.

Harry's in shock, adrenaline pumping, rage shooting through him like a current. He's never laid a hand on another man in all his life, but before he can think he's got the kid like a dog by the scruff of his neck, shoving him out of the restaurant and onto the street. Get the fuck out of here, he spits into his face, get the fuck out.

He doesn't recognize his voice, or his strength. The kid's choking, can't breathe, turning purple as Harry's fingers close in on him. Tourists are stopping to watch.

Angie screams, Harry! and slaps at his arm. Stop, please stop.

He looks at Angie, stops cold, and lets his hand drop. An out of body experience, he's in a daze.

Everybody okay, Angie says, everybody happy.

The kid rubs at his neck as Harry backs away. Fucking TripAdvisor, he says, voice trembling like he's trying not to cry. Just wait, he says, fucking madman.

Inside, Harry looks over at Angie, who's holding her hands over her cheeks, shaking her head.

Harry, baby, she says.

I know, he says, I know.

He sinks onto one of the bar stools and reaches over the counter to grab a bottle. He pours two glasses and she comes over to sit beside him. She should fire him, but she won't. The two of them will grow old together, side by side, marking out time and indifferent years in this island paradise. Harry and Angie, two peas in a pod. It may just be Harry's longest relationship, and he almost laughs at the thought. But no, there's another relationship that will eclipse his and Angie's, at least that's what he's hoping. Once a week, twenty minutes behind a murky glass pane that's never been cleaned. *I love you. I'm waiting for you. Daddy's here.* If he endures, she will too. And then, one day—he can see it—the two of them, him probably a little bent and her a little weathered, arm in arm, boarding a plane. The two of them will go home.

ALL THEM SAVAGES

The baboons took my baby. I know it was them even if no one else wants to believe me. They've been skulking around here for months, sneaking about like thieves, stealing food, throwing the bins over; a few times even cheeky enough to climb in a window to raid the fridge. You know it's them because they like to shit on the floor, mark their territory and tell you who's boss. They're cleverer than people think, more vicious too, with their fangs all sharp and shiny, ready to draw blood. They'll kill you with one bite if they want. They killed my baby. I know it was them.

The others say rubbish, I did it, took the baby, squashed the life out and buried the body somewhere on the mountain. They think I could do that too, no problem, because something's not right in my head. Too much of this, not enough of that. Gertie says don't even listen, it's not your fault. She says I was born like this, came out wrong because my mother drank too much and my father kicked her too many times in the belly when I was inside trying to be alive. Truth is I don't even care. Everyone has something missing, from their soul or their brain or their body, it's not just me.

When I got the baby in my belly, they all went tut-tut and shook their heads and Pa's sister even took me in the car to the clinic in Robertson to have it taken out like a tooth gone black. Won't hurt she said, won't hurt a bit. I didn't care about pain, I cared about ripping a baby out from inside of me. At the clinic I screamed and kicked the nurse in the leg and they shook their heads and told Pa's sister no way, we can't be doing it under these circumstances.

Pa's sister yelled because she likes getting her own way, she said you fucking fools, can't you see she has the brainpower of a child? We got back in the car, she gave me a hand across the face, whack, and I didn't mind because inside I still had the baby brewing softly, softly. A bun in the oven, I always liked that saying because it feels just like that, like there's something delicious cooking in there, just waiting to be ready.

We drove home from the clinic staring anywhere but at each other, and back home they all said okay so who's the father, but obviously you can't tell someone that if you don't know it yourself. Don't get the wrong idea, doesn't mean I'm one of those girls who spread out like butter for any man who comes along, but most of them don't even ask nicely like the men on the TV, bringing flowers and taking their girls for fancy meals in restaurants with candles on the tables and waiters who say yes ma'am to everything. This lot, they just come find me when I'm alone, hanging the washing or preparing the food. They say who's looking pretty today, and start working their hands from the leg all the way up like they're searching for something they lost. They like me because I'm young, nothing yet hanging down to my toes and not enough nerve to slap them away even when I'm tired and want to be left alone. Some of them aren't even so disgusting, some of them kiss me on the neck and try to be gentle when they do their business on top of me. Then I don't mind so much. What I mind is dirty sweaty sticky Mr. V., the boss's father, who visits from time to time to check on things with the workers. Unless the workers live inside my pants there's no check- ing he's doing, but that's how men like him are and there's no changing them and keeping your job in the same breath. That's what Gertie says and she knows best because she's been around here longer than anyone I know. She told me that Mr. V. used to visit her years and years ago when she wasn't yet a grandmother or even a mother. There's talk that Gertie's daughter is one half Mr. V., and that explains how she's doing so well in the city while the rest of us are stuck here like pigs in mud. I don't ask Gertie because she'd tell me if she wanted me to know. Gertie tells me other things, lots of things, like the true fact of how her great-great-grandfather once owned the land around here and how it was taken from him and never returned. That was how it worked, Gertie said, that is the way the world is sometimes, cruel and unfair and full of people hurting other people. You'd think Gertie would be full of hate, but she says hate does nothing but bring more hate and what good would that do. Gertie is the best person I know, she has a laugh that sounds like people clapping, *ha-ha-ha-ha*, and when I hear it, it feels like almost everything else can be forgotten.

It was Gertie those months who looked after me, made Pa's sister buy me vitamins and take me to the clinic for checkups. They took blood and weighed me on the scale or put blue jelly on my belly to listen to the baby's heart. *Doof-doof-doof-doof.* I think it must be the strangest feeling in the world, having two hearts beating in one body. I got big and fat and everything swelled up so I couldn't even fit my own clothes. Gertie dug out some things from her cupboard and gave them to me to wear. I looked in the mirror and didn't know the woman looking back at me, but she smiled and looked happy and I felt like maybe a baby was going to be one of those things that happen in life and make it all better.

When the baby came out it was something fierce, like a bolt of lightning splitting me open from the inside. I screamed and Gertie came running. Pa's sister drove me to the hospital, all the time telling me not to mess in the car. She gave me a dish towel to wedge between my legs and I laughed at her. I'm having a baby not drying plates, I said, but she didn't laugh and in my head I stuck out my tongue at her. Witch. All she wanted anyway was the baby gone out of my body, alive or dead, and she didn't even pretend like dead wasn't the option she'd prefer. At the hospital they took my clothes and tied a white gown around me, and because the pain kept stabbing at me I didn't even care that my underwear were showing to everyone who passed by. They put me in a room and a nurse came by to wrap that strap around my arm. They wrote things down on a chart and told me to lie down in the bed. You bring linen? the nurse asked Pa's sister, and she shook her head. The nurse shrugged her shoulders and said well she'll have to go without, we don't have anything left. Pa's sister told me to get onto the mattress and I saw it had a stain on it dark and rust-colored like blood clotted dry. You'll be okay, she said, and I tried to close the gown so I didn't have to sit too much in the stain. The doctor came and looked between my legs and then another nurse came with her fingers all cold and full of that stuff that's cold like jelly. Hmm and hmm they said and told me it would be a long wait. You can walk around, it will help, the doctor said, but I saw in the waiting room how many women there were heavy with babies waiting to come and I didn't want to lose the bed. Last year Gertie told me a story about how a woman had to give birth standing up because all the hospital beds were full. The baby popped out and she caught it in her very own hands, but because it was full of blood and gunk it slipped through her fingers and onto the hard cement floor. The head it cracked like a coconut, right in two, and I guess the mother wished nothing more than to be dead too.

It took a long, long time before the baby decided to come, I pushed I cried I sweated there in that bloody bed for almost the whole day and night. Just before the sun was ready to come out the baby was too. It pushed its way free, me pushing, it pushing, till together we had it figured out. They took it and put it on me, right on my chest so it could smell me and feel my heart beating *doof-doof-doof*, same as before but this time from the outside. Look, I said to Pa's sister, he's perfect. He took my finger and curled a tiny hand around it and I cooed at him and planted a hundred kisses on his face. Still then I couldn't say who the father was, but only that it wasn't Mr. V. because he would have been the color of caramel then, like Gertie's daughter, and not the color of coffee like he was. They let me sleep that morning and in the evening Pa's sister came back to collect me and the baby and drive us back to the farm. What will you call him? she asked me and I didn't know. You'll think of something, she said, and she gave me a blanket to wrap him in.

When we got back everyone gathered around to meet the baby, some even brought presents for him. Gertie was the one I handed him to, I said here boy, meet your Ouma because there wasn't anyone but Gertie and me to love him proper. Gertie held him up and looked him up and down and let him nestle against her. Look at you clever girl, she said to me, look what a perfect child you have brought into this world. It was true, he was beautiful, the baby, the most beautiful thing I ever saw and the only thing I ever had that was mine. It made me feel good that I made him and carried him and that my something-missing brain could think straight enough to look after him good and proper the way a mother should. I fed him from my breasts and washed him gently in the kitchen sink holding his tiny head upright and I rocked him to sleep in my arms. Every night I looked down at him in the bed next to me and I said thank you God because how else did such luck come to be mine?

Luck! Hah, luck is like the devil, sneaky and cruel. Every day it gets dished out like porridge at breakfast, some days there's a big bowl in front of you and other days you go hungry. The day it happened, the baby was outside in a crib just like Moses from the Bible, sleeping sweet and sound in the fresh spring air because Gertie told me fresh air is better for a baby than inside air. I wasn't far from where he lay, hanging the sheets in the sun, singing because the radio was on and that song I like about the girl saying good-bye to her old boyfriend was playing and there was no one around to tell me shush you're breaking my ears like usual. The baby was peaceful like an angel, full of goodness and warm milk and making that curled up face while he slept that could have been dreams or wind. It was Mr. V. who came by then and took me inside with him for the not so long time it takes him to do what he does. Grunt, grunt, grunt, roll over, catch his breath. It's always the same so I know how many minutes to count on the clock before it's over. He hadn't been with me since the baby came and he looked at me down there like something was in the wrong place. They cut you or was it a natural birth? he asked. Natural, I said and he nodded like he knew the answer already. There are exercises, he said, you can do them to tighten up again. I laughed at him because he had some cheek telling me to exercise my parts when he smelled always stale with coffee and cigarettes and had skin oily like a mackerel. Yes *baas*, I said, I'll get nice and tight. He didn't ask to see the baby and I guess he wasn't worried it might be his. I wanted badly to take a shower but the water restrictions on the farm say it's once a day and nothing besides or they'll dock the workers' pay. Instead I took one of the baby's wet wipes and scooped his stuff out of me just the same way I would clean up the baby after it made a mess in its nappy.

No present, *baas*? I said when I finished, because sometimes he brings me something nice like a chocolate or a soap, but I have to remind him or his old man memory forgets to give it. He had nothing, but he said next time, and dressed in his clothes before leaving the same way as he came. I drank some juice from the fridge and went back outside to the baby and the washing and that's when I saw the crib empty like a hole in the ground. The scream that came out of me was from someone else because the voice wasn't mine but the terrible sick want-to-die feeling was. I ran around the place looking under chairs and in the bushes but the baby couldn't walk or crawl and it made no sense that it would be anywhere but where I left him, tucked into the crib. I heard the baboons then, cackling away in the tall, tall trees, laughing at me, and I knew it was them, thieving vicious creatures full of spite and nothing else. I tried following the cries, ran behind the house into the mountains, cutting my bare feet on rocks and branches that made me spurt blood but feel no pain because all that pained me was my heart and my fear and the terribleness of being without my baby. The baboons aren't just devious they're clever too, because I could hear them but not see them. I suppose they were hiding somewhere, devouring the baby, ripping his legs, his arms, his little head to pieces, clothes still on him and not even a chance to cry out for his mother to come save him. I screamed and I screamed and I screamed until the sound couldn't even come out anymore. My face was wet with tears, the *doof-doof-doof* of my heart in my throat made me want to be sick and I vomited onto the ground at my bloody feet.

I shook my head and went back to the crib to look again because maybe I was crazy and it hadn't even happened at all. But the crib was still empty and the sick feeling was still there and there was no one to help and nothing I could do but sob the tears clean out of my body. I sat at the crib holding the baby's blanket, smelling his smell, trying to make it all be a dream. Eventually, the sun went down and the day turned its back on me like everything else. The voices I heard first were Ezra and Derrick, back from the farm with empty lunch packets and filthy overalls. I tried my voice for the first time since the screaming and it scratched out the words. Help me, I said. Help me. They came over to where I was sitting with the crib and I told them the baboons took the baby and they looked at each other and looked at me and said oh, what have you done? I said it again, the baboons took my baby, I cried it out this time and still they just looked at me like I was a different kind of crazy to the normal kind of crazy they're used to. Please, I said and I hit my fists into Ezra's chest because he was standing there like a stone not moving to help me or hold me or hear my story. Please, I cried, and said it again and again and again until he took me and held me still.

The others soon came back, everyone gathered round and whispered and pointed and I could tell that no one, not even one, believed me. Derrick, because he's sometimes nice to me and maybe because he thinks he could have been the father of the baby, said okay, okay and took a flashlight and headed off into the mountains to go and look. He came back twenty minutes later, said sorry, nothing to be found, but he smelled of smoke and I think he just went to have a cigarette somewhere quiet. I screamed into the night sky and said it again, the baboons took my baby, and everyone just shook their heads at me. Pa's sister she came up to me then and slapped me across the face to stop the crying. This is why, she spat, this is why I didn't want you having it in the first place. The men started saying they were hungry, it was dinnertime, and some of them went into their houses to eat like it was just another night and all that was missing was some laundry from the line. Some of the women stayed outside with me. They kept saying, what happened you can tell us just tell us, and again and again I said it and saw in their faces that they thought every word coming out of me was a lie. The looks they shot at me through suspicious eyes might as well have been knives. No, knives would have been better, the pain is sharp and quick, in and out. Maybe they're all just too used to dead children, the ones left raped and sliced on the dump, discarded like old shoes. Ezra's niece was taken last year, gang-raped and set alight, but she just wouldn't die, lived for six months more in a hospital room with tubes coming in and out of her and no skin left covering her bones. That's this place, or maybe the whole world: cruel like you wouldn't believe. Cruel like you hope you never find out.

When Gertie came back from the late shift she took me in her arms and I let the tears soak her dress and she said, there, there my girl, Gertie is here. I told her the story and she said, tell it again, and I told it again. She looked outside at the crib and walked around the house slowly with a funny look on her face like she was talking to herself in her head. She said, tell me one more time and after I did she nodded her head. Those baboons, she said, they will take anything. I cried fresh tears and Gertie said come come, you will need your strength for tomorrow. She put me to bed in her house, gave me two big tablets white and chalky that she said would take away the pain for the night. I fell to a sleep so heavy I thought I was dead but the morning came anyway and I was sorry to wake up. My breasts hurt from the milk wanting to get out and I squeezed at them and wiped the liquid on a kitchen towel. Gertie had to go to work but she gave me more of the white tablets and said, sleep, sleep and so I did. In the afternoon I woke again with my throat dry like the peeling walls of the bedroom and a head throbbing like a heart. I was still in Gertie's house and I wandered around, looking at the things that were familiar because Gertie just about raised me. When my father died, stabbed through the liver and the heart and the head by another picker on the farm, his house went to me because there wasn't anyone else around to want it. I had no money but Gertie helped me make things nice and pretty, stitched yellow covers for the old falling-apart cushions and hung lace curtains on the windows that she'd made from cutting up an old tablecloth. She was clever like that. I looked at the photographs on Gertie's table, her daughter from the city smiling and looking like she never worked a day in a field on a farm. Gertie was proud of that, it was her hard work making sure her daughter went to school and then to university. She was pretty, nice teeth, hair almost straight. I used to be jealous of her for being Gertie's real daughter but then Gertie told me I was her farm daughter with just as big a place in her heart and then I felt okay.

I wanted to go back to my house, to smell the baby's things and drink from the secret bottle under the sink that Derrick gave me once. To loosen you up, is what he said but he was the one talking funny after he drank from it. Still it made me feel warm inside when I had a glass of it, the taste was foul and sharp but afterward it tickled me like feathers in my belly. Inside the house, I checked around and still the baby was gone and still from outside in the trees I could hear the baboons laughing at me, not one bit sorry for what they'd done, just cackling away like they'd won and I'd lost. The day came and went in a blur, sleep was the only thing that passed the time without letting the pain rip my insides apart. In the evening, there was a knock at the door and Mary standing outside said, come see. They had made a small grave in the garden and stuck a cross in the ground and put some flowers around it. A nice gesture, Gertie would say, but really they just wanted me shut up, causing no trouble, making no reason for the *baas* to come by and start asking questions. I said thank you because you're meant to say thank you even when what you feel is the furthest thing from thankful that there is. I sat at the grave and wept and thought everything good was gone forever. Gertie called me in later to eat something and I pushed food around on a plate before she gave me more of the white tablets and put me to bed.

Every day now is the same, the very same. The milk is gone, my breasts dried and shriveled back to the way they were before. Gertie said to put away the baby's things, so they're in a box in the bottom of the cupboard and the only thing to say the baby was there at all. Some days I think it was all a great big trick my mind played on me, but how could anyone's mind want to do that. I think about the baby every minute my eyes are open, I think about his smile and the two little teeth that were growing in his mouth like pips and the way he held a hand to my chest when I fed him milk and the way he smelled in the morning after his breakfast, and then I think about the last day and him being all alone and how the baboons took him and how he is gone forever and how I don't even have a tiny little piece of him left to bury or weep over, no bones no hair no flesh to turn to ashes and dust like it says in the Bible. Nothing, not one thing besides my own sorry tears.

The Sunday after it happened, Pastor Dan came to see me. He said, if there's anything you want to confess, God is always ready to listen. I wish you could tell a pastor to *voetsek* but instead I told him the story and asked him if baboons went to hell. He looked at me and shook his head and said, if you change your mind you know where to find me. He blessed the grave and said a prayer and whispered to some of the others. Then he took a plate of Gertie's biscuits home with him for his tea. I curled up on the bed and tried to sleep through the noise of everyone drinking their Sunday out of a bottle. Weeks after that, Mr. V. was back. He came to find me while I was standing over the sink peeling carrots for a stew. His hands started their creeping and I gripped my fingers around the knife in my hand nice and tight. Oh, I thought, I could do this and not be one bit sorry, not one bit afraid of God's punishment or going to hell. This is what happens when the worst thing that can happen already happened to you. Stop, I said but his hands kept working their way up my dress, up and under and taking handfuls of flesh like they belonged to him and not me. Stop, I said again, this time loud like a bark and he stopped and breathed into my ear a few moments, wondering what to do next. I stood still, dead still, hand on the knife, and then I heard his breath getting further away and his footsteps tip-tapping on the tiles as he left. It felt good, the closest to good I felt since the baby got taken into the trees.

Most days now I go walking in the mountains behind the houses, looking to find something but I don't even know what. Bones maybe, even clothes. I feel like a detective on the TV, searching for clues, but what justice will I ever find in a baboon. Days I come too close to the troop, the baboons bare their teeth and do their best to frighten me away. I scream at them, top of my lungs, let out all the sad and angry and bitter and wave my arms at them like a madwoman. I hate you, I scream, I hate you, and it scares me sometimes how strong that feeling is. Usually they run off, up the trees to cackle at me and remind me that they couldn't care less about my pain.

I remember when the baboons first started coming down off the mountains and into the houses. Everyone cursed them, moaned at the mess they left behind and all the trouble they caused. Gertie told me it wasn't their fault. We've taken their land, she said, they just want food. They just want to make a home. But the *baas* had their land now. He built a bigger fence around his house, and put that electric stuff around the crop fields to keep them out of the vineyards and away from the grapes. Sometimes there would be a dead sheep or a dead dog in the morning and the boys would have to clean up the blood and guts lying all over like a spilled dinner pot.

Last year, Ezra shot the leader of the troop, a huge bully of a male with an eye missing from a fight. Two bullets he sank into his chest before the animal fell to the ground, loud and heavy. The blood was dark and thick like ours, oozing out of the wound and onto the grass. The baboon's expression made it look like he was in the worst pain or maybe just sad to be dying, but he clutched at his chest and made a strange gurgling noise that reminded me of my father on his dying day, the life seeping slowly from him with the blood. The other baboons watched from the trees. They howled and cried, in anger and mourning, just like people, and I felt sorry for them because they weren't doing anything except be baboons. Ezra took the meat and sold it to Justice, the caretaker of the next-door farm who comes from the Congo and likes bush meat more than chicken. I wanted to ask him what baboon tasted like but I never got a chance.

In any case, now I don't feel one bit sorry for the baboons, not one bit. I only feel sorry for me and for the baby, snatched from his crib and chewed up like he wasn't anything more than a scrap of meat. In church they say Jesus likes you to forgive, but my heart has no place for forgiveness. It's too broken for that. What I want is the bad thing, the thing Pastor Dan says is the Devil's business and not ours. But I think it is the only thing that will make it better, that will balance out the bad. Yes, what I want is revenge. I want to hold a baboon in my hands, I want to slice it open, rip out its heart, hang its bloodstained teeth around my neck like a warrior and leave its body to rot in the sun for all to see. I want it to bleed like my baby bled, feel pain like my pain. I want it to die slow and wretched, with not one flicker of mercy. Yes, that's what I want. Maybe after it's done I'll feel no different, just the same empty bit of flesh and bone. But maybe I'll feel better, stronger, like I'm in charge for once. That would be a good feeling I think.

Some nights, when the boys are feeling political, they'll sit around and talk about taking what's theirs, standing up to the *baas* and the system and this messed-up world where nobody is anything but a slave most of the time, bending and scraping at the mercy of the ones with all the power and all the money and all the know-how. This country, they say, you fight and fight for freedom and just when you get it at last, you realize that what you get is only more of the same, dressed up in different clothes but underneath it all, nothing different than before. Yes, they shout, our time has come. We are the future. This is where things change. Fighting words, angry words, but the anger doesn't go anywhere but out into the night air with the mosquitoes. Come the morning, they've lost it all in a bottle or a fight or a woman. Then just like that, the fire is gone and it's back to yes *baas*, no *baas*, anything you say *baas*. Nothing changes, nobody is anything they weren't before. Me, I'm different. My anger's got nowhere to go but here: waiting, watching, biding my time till I can be the one doing the taking instead of the one losing out. It's coming, I know it, I feel it. Watch your back, savages, I say. I'm coming for you.

HONOR LIFE LONG
WITH TEARS

Here's the thing about Berlin: absolutely anything goes. The stranger, the more perverse, the more outside the realm of so-called normal, the better. Swingers, bears, submissives, fetishists, there's a bar and a club for all; an underground room or a secret door, even a Facebook page. You want it, whatever it is, whatever you can think of, and it's here, somewhere. The city throbs with sex, with deviance. If you're an outsider, you're in, firm and fast. This is what he was here for, this is what he was after. Not wildness, not permissiveness. Only acceptance. It was his mother's idea—his fucking mother who suggested it. She couldn't take it anymore, the suicide attempts, the depression, the countless failed sessions at therapy. She'd read an article on the Internet, she printed it out and showed it to him.

Look, she'd said, it might not be what you're looking for, but it can't be any worse.

It was true, there wasn't much that could be worse. She paid for the ticket, one-way from Dublin, and drove him to the airport the next week.

Berlin, it was another thing on a long list of things to try, most of them suggested by his mother or his therapist. He wasn't averse to trying, only weary of the inevitable disappointment that came as a result. Because no matter how much yoga you do, no matter how Zen your inner mind, no matter how stimulated you are by learning another language, a crippling deformity is still a crippling deformity. Zara, the therapist, liked to tell him that manhood was a much broader concept than genitals. Of course, that would be true if he didn't have a fucking micropenis, a minuscule knob of flesh in place of a nice fat workable cock. Actually, he'd stood up when Zara said it, pulled down his jeans, and revealed himself to her.

Look, he said. Look at this and tell me how little this has to do with my sense of manhood.

She looked away, maybe in revulsion, maybe out of politeness.

No, actually: it would have to be revulsion. That was the standard response, and in all honesty he couldn't blame anyone for it.

You want to believe the world is fair in its distribution of luck and fortune, but nothing could be further from the truth. Some people have all the luck. Others have none. Sure, he wasn't born in a war zone, he wasn't a quadriplegic, he didn't have severe brain damage. He could live a relatively normal life, he'd gone to a good school, studied afterward at Trinity, taken a gap year and seen some of the world. He had a decently paying job and an apartment in Rathmines, he shopped for groceries at Dunnes and went to the pub on Friday nights with his mates, who speculated occasionally among themselves as to whether or not he might be gay. Miraculously, over twelve years at Wesley College he never once had to reveal his naked self to any of his classmates. His mother had spoken to the headmaster, who in turn invented a lung disease that prevented him from taking part in sports. He was a little doughy as a result, not helped by the sloping shoulders inherited from his grandfather, but still it was preferable to the alternative.

Shame, shame is a heavy burden to carry. It weighs you down, it stays close like a shadow, never out of reach of the rest of you. He avoided mirrors, avoided looking or touching. He showered quickly, never took a bath. Dressed with his eyes to the ceiling. It made his stomach turn over double every time he caught a glance, a sinking feeling, the realization that it was still there and would always be. Jesus loves you just the way you are, is what the priest told him by way of encouragement or explanation. He stopped going to church after that, and his mother no longer tried to persuade him that it would do him good.

All his childhood, he'd been blissfully unaware of anything being different with his body. It was only from around five or six that he started overhearing his father.

Jesus, Triona, he'd say, it's not normal for it to be that tiny, surely.

No, it wasn't normal, and it didn't grow any bigger. The doctor—geriatric Dr. Byrne in his Dalkey practice—he'd never seen anything like it and spent twelve years telling them it would come into its own. It was Ireland in the eighties, this was not within the frame of reference. His parents took the doctor's word for it and waited patiently as the years passed. When his mother bathed him she'd avert her eyes and tell him to use the washcloth while she readied the towel. Then one Christmas holiday when he was eight, his father nearly died of shame and it dawned on him that all was not okay with his body. They'd been staying in Cork at his grandparents' house, all the cousins and uncles and aunts crammed in and the kids bunking down on mattresses in the living room. He'd wet the bed one night, taken off his pajamas, and gone into the kitchen where the adults were gathered round drinking tea.

Sweet baby Jesus, his uncle Harry said.

His father jumped up from his chair and pulled him out of the room by the scruff of his neck.

We don't all need to see your disgusting little knob, Robbie! he screamed, his voice high-pitched and his eyes burning with tears.

He could hear his mother in the kitchen crying as his father scrubbed him down in the bath, ice-cold water and soap and his rough hands pummeling his flesh like he wanted to erase it altogether.

It was an accident, Da, he said, crying because suddenly it seemed like he'd done a lot more than wet the sheets.

His father lifted him out of the tub and wrapped him in a towel and then pulled him close, squeezing him as he sobbed against his scrawny chest.

It's okay, son, he said; it's okay. It will all be okay.

They tried, his parents, they really tried. Did whatever they could to avoid focusing on his genitals, the great elephant in the room. At the seaside, he knew instinctively not to change in front of the other boys, not to show himself. He became furtive, a natural at eight—able to slip by undetected and unrevealed. The anxiety was immense, the panic always just there, under the surface, waiting. Who would see, who would find out. At thirteen the other lads started developing hair, their voices deepened and their bodies changed. All they could talk about was their cocks.

You don't want it too big, like, Andrew warned, the girls can't fit it inside their gee.

Finn was a redhead, the others wanted to see if the curtains matched the drapes.

Feck off, he said, but he pulled his shorts down all the same and showed off the thatch of copper hair that was beginning to grow.

Boys, teenagers, full of raging hormones and the excitement of their pending transition into manhood. Hand jobs, blow jobs, full on fucking, all of it lay ahead, the great paradise of the future. But not for him.

He was a nice guy, that was the problem. Not bad looking either, apart from the shoulders and a few pimples. The girls liked him. Miraculously, he could manage to talk to them even though his friends with their regular-sized penises clammed up or behaved like morons. He found himself with a girlfriend when he was fifteen. She invited him back to her place while her mother was at work and they lay on her sheets and kissed. She moaned softly, like she'd seen them do on the TV. She moved a hand from his chest down to his trousers, her hand searching for the bulge. The bulge! There would never be a bulge. Even when he was erect there was little more than a pitiful thumb-sized protrusion; hardly worth the effort. He moved her hand away quickly.

We should go slow, Cynthia, he said, I don't want to pressure you into doing something you're not ready to do.

It worked a trick, she sighed and relaxed and they spent the rest of the afternoon playing table tennis in her garage. They stayed together a month or so more and then when she decided she wanted to do more with him in her bed than kiss, he broke it off.

She sobbed, is it someone else?

He shrugged. Maybe, he said.

At Wesley, he got a reputation then as a player, a bit of a lothario. It was almost laughable, but he played along, used it as cover. There were a few more girlfriends over the years, all of them dispensed with just in time. It wasn't that he didn't want to have sex with them, he just couldn't imagine how it might work. He'd seen one of Andrew's condoms, he'd looked at the magazines in the newsagents' and watched the films. There wasn't much he could do with what he had, that he knew for sure.

Long hours he spent weeping in his mother's arms as she stroked his cheek and said, there, there son. Everyone is damaged, everyone in this world, she said. You just can't always see it.

She told him to be a good man, to be a gentle man and a kind one. The rest will follow, she promised, every pot has a lid. She had no shortage of platitudes. Love, she said, love is not about skin and bones, it's about heart. She wanted to believe it too, that he might somehow overcome his challenge, as she called it. His father, he struggled with it, with the physical fact of that misshapen thing attached to his son's groin. He couldn't look at him naked—could hardly look him in the eye in fact. He was a generation of football and Guinness, not much besides. There was no way of connecting with his son if his son was not a proper boy, one of the lads, chasing girls and having the *craic*.

Robbie, Jesus, he'd say, you want to lighten up, a long face is worse than a short mickey. He said it when he was drunk and apologized after but the sting didn't leave his son then or ever, only drew him further away.

On his gap year he fell in love, wholly and completely. Her name was Lucy, he met her on the bus between Hoi An and Da Nang. When the bus broke down, they were stranded in the middle of nowhere, just the two of them and three dozen Vietnamese locals.

They ushered them to a small hotel by the side of the highway and told them the bus would come the next morning to take them on their way. He and Lucy spoke all night, she was beautiful and smart and funny and the first woman whom he could look at without feeling the panic rise in his chest. Two weeks they spent together, learning each other inside out, starting to finish each other's sentences. One night, they lay together on the bed and she took off all her clothes.

Now you, she said, when she was naked, shining like a sliver of the moon.

What possessed him, he'll never know, but he stripped off his clothes, shirt and shorts and then his underwear, and in that moment, that terrible moment when her eyes took it in and told him everything he needed to know, he realized that there was no going back. She tried to smile, bless her heart, tried to make out like she didn't want to throw up or run from the room.

Come here, she said, come lie here with me.

Her voice was shaky, she looked like she might cry.

We don't have to, he said. I'm sorry, I probably should have warned you or something. You know, prepared you for the disappointment.

She was a kindhearted girl and she shook her head, no, no, she said. I'm not disappointed. It's still you.

But it wasn't, it wasn't still him, because he was two people, the man with his clothes on, and the freak with them off. They tried, he lay on top of her and tried to maneuver himself inside her.

Maybe this way, she said, and they shifted position a few times.

In the end, she said she was tired and they stopped. He lay behind her and pulled her close, so that his face was in her hair and his breath warm against her neck. He held her, held on for dear life, because he knew she'd be gone in the morning.

Berlin he decided would be the last great hope, the final attempt. If he couldn't make it work, by which he meant, if he could not make a life that was bearable—he would call it a day. Buy a fat wad of some or other drug, ingest it, wait for it all to end. He'd post his mother a farewell letter, he'd arrange his affairs so that she would be looked after. But he'd stop fighting to make a go of this pathetic excuse for a life. He hated Stephen Hawking, hated every fucker who triumphed over gross bodily deformity and disease. What were they saying to the world, what message were they sending? Whatever it was, it didn't apply to him, it didn't apply to anyone with a fucking micromanhood.

Online, he found a community for the similarly afflicted, the men with maimed or microversions of penises. There were enough to make him feel mildly better, but only just. Sam, fucking Sam, he was full of good cheer and hot tips like Learning to Please without Penetration. He had a wife and a mistress, allegedly, both of whom referred to his cock as Their Turn-On Button. Fucking liar, Robbie thought, but he read the forum religiously nonetheless. There was Burt, penis removed after a botched circumcision; Luther, like him with a micropenis; Dave C., the nullo who'd had his removed by choice; Dave P., who'd lost his to a sliding door as a child; Andy, who was so morbidly obese that his cock had been retracted into his belly; and a handful of others who kept the threads going. Dave P. had had reconstructive surgery more than eight times, each one resulting in his new cock turning black and falling off of its own accord. Last year, he ditched the penis and found Jesus. God loves us as we are, he liked to write. We are all beautiful creatures of the Lord!!!

Robbie had been to a surgeon in London once, researched it over the Internet and booked a trip to hear what his options might be. The surgeon had him naked on the table, feeling around his bits, prodding, poking.

Yes, he said, this is a severe case.

He finished his examination and they returned to his desk. Look, he said, let me be frank. There's almost no tissue there. Not much to attach to. These cases . . . they tend not to work out like you hope. What I mean is, say it all goes well, the phallus attaches, you have some bulk. Even presuming the best-case scenario, it's unlikely it will function.

In the end he decided against it, reckoned some feeling might be better than none at all. At least there was that, the ability to self-pleasure, those desperate encounters under the covers, the loathing of his flesh only briefly eclipsed by its ability to yield pleasure.

Dave C., his advice was to find the fetishists, the gays, the dominant women, the sexual perverts.

You wouldn't believe what people are into, he wrote.

Course, he wasn't living in south Dublin, doing brunch at Avoca and Bon Iver concerts at Vicar Street. In Dublin, homosexuality was still the height of conceivable perversion; there wasn't scope for much more. It wasn't what his mother said in so many words when she'd suggested Berlin, but he supposed it was what she'd meant all the same. Maybe you'll feel freer to, er, explore your options, she said.

Bless her. Jesus, what it must have been like for her, willing her son out into a world of sexual deviance; anything to make him less alone in the world.

He started off full of big plans. Say yes to everything. Try anything. Experiment. Explore. He went to clubs, to gatherings in basements and house parties and underground affairs in abandoned buildings and theme parks. He met trannies and latex-clad men with whips and women with beards; he met men who admitted openly to fucking their dogs, swingers and porn stars and a roaring queen with glitter in his beard and horns implanted into his forehead. It was dizzying, the spread of humanity, the sheer scope of weirdness and permissiveness, the endless availability of options. He went home with one man and sucked off another in a bar in Kreuzberg called The Glory Hole. He went to Berghain, took the pills offered to him, danced till dawn with his shirt off and the sweat dripping off him as the music pumped and the crowd around him lost themselves in various states of drug-, drink-, or rhythm-induced euphoria. A couple approached him sometime around two P.M. the next day when the crowd began to thin, bought him an ice cream cone from the bar, and asked if he'd like a blow job. Because it was

Berlin and because he'd been dancing for fifteen hours straight and because this was the point of him being here, he said, sure, why not. They went behind the dance floor, to the darkened concrete seats that were like something out of a Fellini movie. The music, intoxicating, vibrating right through him, took away his nerve and he said, I should warn you, I have a small problem. The couple was German, they took turns putting their hands inside his jeans and then their mouths around his cock. They laughed, but not unkindly, it was a fascination. Afterward, they exchanged numbers and invited him on a day trip to Potsdam. His shame lifted, the world suddenly seemed less awful a place. There were more encounters, some pleasant, some terrifying. He took more drugs than he should, drank and smoked and existed on almost no sleep. Three months in, and every encounter became the same, empty, weightless. When he was neither drunk nor high he could see that it wasn't what he wanted. He was not gay, was not interested in being someone's bitch, role-playing that he was a child with a woman who fantasized about fucking young boys. What he wanted was love, the love of a woman, the beauty of something intimate and achingly, achingly real. In the bakery, he found a flyer for a seminar called Closing The Wound, took a train to Cologne one weekend, and sat cross-legged with twelve other people around an aging Californian Jew who called himself Shankar and wore his gray hair in a long plait on the side of his head. Over the course of three days, they hugged and wept and spoke of the fragility of their frightened inner child and danced like men and women possessed with their arms in the air and their heads thrown back. He met an Englishman, Tom, who was well versed in the jargon of wounds and centeredness. In the group sharing session he told them how his mother had left three sisters and himself behind in London to take up with a French woman she'd met on a plane coming back from her sister's funeral. Actually, Tom confessed to him later, he was really only there to meet women. On the last day, he pocketed the numbers of two young Danish students and Mira, the gray-haired Belgian widow with two-colored eyes.

He stopped going out, stayed in and read books and took long walks around the city. Everywhere there were signs of the past, the war and the wall, death and scarring all marked out on the streets. The future too, taking shape by the day: Turkish grocers and shi-sha lounges, Korean restaurants, Russian bars, American diners, a melting pot of all the world. He took a job at a shipping company, donned a suit by day, and at night ate dinner with his colleague Jens or alone at the bistro on the corner of his street. Jens was in his forties, divorced, balding, a little fat in the gut. He was mildly obsessed with Tinder, went on dates as often as he could, although most of the women aborted the relationship after the first dismal drink.

How about you, he said, dating?

He shook his head, no, not yet.

He invented a story of a long and complicated heartbreak, a betrayal, a devastation of the worst kind. Jens, feeling confessional, had told him the story of his grandfather Andreas, a Nazi who along with a fellow officer called Michael had evaded prison at the end of the war by slicing the SS tattoo out of his flesh with a pocketknife.

He spent his life claiming that the scar under his arm was from a bullet wound, Jens said. It was only after he died that we found his diaries. He had written it all down, everything he'd done, all his shame on those pages. Names, letters. There was a postcard among the pages, sent from South Africa. *Wurden wir mit dem Leben belohnt oder bestraft?* Were we rewarded with life or punished with it?

From Michael? he asked, and Jens shrugged.

One must assume that is where he ended up.

Everyone carries a secret, a shame we cannot imagine. But still, Jens said, he got away with it.

His eyes were gleaming, maybe proud, maybe a little awestruck.

He married his neighbor, can you believe it? A young Jew who survived the camps. She had no money, no family still alive. He was all she had to anchor her to life. So she agreed to be his wife. They were not even altogether unhappy, Jens said, they loved each other in the end, because to survive something is to claim victory over death.

Jens was the only German he knew who wanted to talk about the war. He took him on a tour of Berlin's bunkers.

Did you know Hitler was chronically flatulent? he said. Can you imagine being in a bunker with him? Death by gas one way or the other!

At the bistro, there was a waitress, fiercely dark-skinned, black-eyed. She always looked mildly terrified, but smiled nonetheless and took his order in a soft voice accented with French. He wondered about her, wondered how she'd come to be here and why. He wanted to ask, but she appeared to be so painfully uncomfortable with her own shadow that he didn't. Every few nights, he'd see her, smile, order his food, leave her a handsome tip. He liked the way she walked, head high, back straight, stride long and smooth. He imagined what she would look like naked, spread against the white sheets like a shadow. He wanted to know her; he didn't know why.

He bumped into her one Saturday at the Turkish grocer's. He was buying eggs and she was picking out greens.

Hi, he said, hello.

He went over to her and she looked blankly at him.

From the restaurant, he said, er, you're the waitress?

She nodded but didn't smile. Yes, she said.

Would you like to get a coffee? he said, I was about to get one.

No, she said, I have to go to work.

Maybe tomorrow? he said.

I have to work, she replied.

But the restaurant's closed on Mondays, he said.

She let out a little laugh then and covered her mouth with her hand.

See? he said. I make you laugh.

He didn't know why he was pushing so hard, only that he felt some strange kinship with her. They met the next evening, drank coffee, and split a thick slice of carrot cake. She picked out the raisins and put them in a little pile on the side of the plate. She said very little, but he was happy to sit with her and watch her and wonder about the thoughts inside her head.

Where are you from? he asked.

Far away, she said. She ate her cake, took out the raisins, sipped from her cup.

I'm from Ireland, he said.

I know, she replied, your accent.

They were indoors but her thick winter coat was still on.

You're not too warm? he asked.

She shook her head, I am always cold here.

Her phone rang and she answered in a language he couldn't make out. She sounded angry but when she put the phone away she smiled.

My friend, she explained.

So, he said, what brought you to Berlin?

She leaned forward, narrowed her eyes. You want to know how I came here? she said. He nodded, yes.

Alright, she said. Then let me tell you. I came on a boat. You know the ones you see in the news? One like that. Four hundred of us, hiding below deck. Ones who die, they throw overboard, like a banana peel. But, she said, we were lucky. We did not sink. We did not get turned back. In Italy, I had six months in a detention center. Then to Germany. Three years waiting for papers, waiting in queues at the *Ausländerbehörde*. *Ausländer*. Aliens, like we come from outer space. There is a crazy woman who goes there every day to walk the corridors. She shouts at the top of her voice, go home smelly people. Go home all you ugly black apes. We sit and look at our hands. No one tells her to leave.

I'm sorry, he said. I am so sorry.

Why are you sorry? she said. I am here. I am alive. This is a good story.

Her name was Dembe. He said it aloud and it sounded like music. They began to meet once a week, on a Monday evening. He suggested going for dinner but she only wanted cake. He told her about Dublin, put on a Northside accent to amuse her, and explained to her the rules of hurling. She told him, but slowly and only in bite-sized portions, about her life. Where she'd been born, the war that had ravaged the country village by village, the refugee camp she'd been sent to with her brother when the two of them were the only ones left alive. She told him about her grandmother, her hands so gnarled and bent from working the fields that she couldn't close them, but her heart big enough to take in all the swollen-bellied children without mothers. She did not tell him about the men who came to the camp, the ones who raped the girls and sliced the hands off the men who tried to defend them; she didn't tell him how she almost died from the violence done to her body, or that her uterus had been left in a heap on the ground where the soldiers had taken her. Some things could not be said aloud.

Her voice he could listen to for hours, the timbre of it, the way she urged the words out as though they were reluctant to leave the safety of her mouth. She was far from beautiful but everything that was beautiful. He looked at her, wanted to be the man who could love her back from the terribleness of her life. He wanted her to love him too and so he put on his best self in her company.

Do you like movies? he said.

She did, and he took her the next week. Bought her a bucket of popcorn, which she did not touch, and a Coke, which she slipped into her handbag. He wondered if she was desperately poor, hungry, maybe living in a room with twelve other people. He was afraid to ask.

Are you happy, he said, are you happy here?

She looked at her hands. Here? she said. I should be happy here.

But are you? he said, and she looked away.

They went to the Jewish Museum, walked through the strange and disquieting building of empty rooms and dead ends; peered into glass cabinets containing letters and spectacles and the shoes of the dead. He wanted to take her hand, to share in the overwhelming intake of tragedy, but she kept her arms folded tight across her chest. Another time, they went to an exhibition of memento mori, examined skulls carved from ivory and coffins in miniature, carved altars and jewelry made from the bones of the dead. There was a necklace with a pendant, a tiny coffin with a skeleton secreted away inside. Carved into the coffin, the words *I will honor life/long with tears/LLHZ/Your memory far too dear*, a tribute from a son to his father.

I like this, Dembe said, I like this best of all.

Why? he asked, and she smiled.

Because it shows grief to be beautiful.

He wanted to kiss her and she must have seen it because she turned and walked briskly away. He caught his heart in his hands and followed her out of the gallery onto the street.

He spoke to his parents once a week and his mother always asked the same question.

Are you finding your feet, love?

She would be sitting in his old bedroom, converted now into a computer room, his old Smashing Pumpkins posters replaced with prints of the Connemara coastline that they'd bought on their last trip to the west of Ireland.

The only part worth visiting, his father always grumbled. Dublin, Dublin's gone to shite. His mother waited for his father to leave the room and then she leaned into the screen and whispered, so you've made some friends have you?

He wanted to tell her about Dembe, to reassure her that he was feeling something resembling the opposite of desolation for the first time in years, he wanted to give her that much to hold on to. But he was terrified, terrified that if he uttered the words aloud they might make her disappear into the realm of some imagined world, that he would lose her instantly.

I'm happy, Ma, he said. I think I'm really happy here.

She dabbed at her eyes and nodded. Okay, she said, okay.

Come, Dembe said.

It was a rare Sunday that she had off from work. I want to take you somewhere today. They went to Görlitzer Park. He'd been once before, after a heavy night out; passed out next to a child's birthday party and awoke to find someone's pug licking his foot.

Dembe led him past the parents with strollers and the joggers and the dog walkers, past a busker singing horribly off-key and a girl setting up a tightrope between two trees. It was cold, she pulled her coat tightly around her and he saw how poorly it fit her. A donation or an Oxfam buy, he thought. Two men spotted them and came running, smiling wide, calling out something. One lifted Dembe up in his arms, twirled her around, said something in that language and made her laugh. The men were dark, much darker than Dembe, tall and lithe and both of them in sneakers bright white and new. Dealers, he realized, that's what they were.

These are my brothers, Malik and Sutay, Dembe said. Asylum brothers.

They laughed, Dembe and the men, and he watched how they were together, easy and intimate and familiar.

We go to German class together, she explained. Together we learn to become German. He didn't know what to say, what to do. He tried to relax, to smile.

Why don't we go get a drink? he said.

The men laughed and said something to each other.

Malik smiled. Thank you, he said, but we are Muslims, and today we are working.

Sorry, he said. I'm sorry.

Christ, he felt more out of his depth than he had at some of the fetish clubs he'd frequented when he first arrived in the city. Sutay said something and Dembe translated. He said you should come for dinner. They will cook.

He smiled, that will be great, he said, I'd love that.

The men shook his hand and laughed at him when he messed up the handshake.

It's okay, Malik said, we practice.

He took Dembe to a restaurant on the other side of the park and they sat and ate burgers and watched the people come and go.

Do you know them from home? he asked her.

No, she said. They are Gambians. We met at the school. They are still waiting for papers. That is why they sell drugs in the park.

There is nothing else for them to do. The government will not let them get jobs.

He watched her eat her burger, first pulling the bun apart with her fingers and eating it like a bird, then cutting the meat with her fork.

They send money home every month, this money they make here. It goes home, feeds ten brothers and sisters. It is why they come here. To make a better life for everyone.

He wiped his hands on a napkin and hoped there was no ketch-up on his face.

They sound like good brothers, he said, and she smiled.

Yes, she said. They are my family here.

Again, he wanted to take her hand, to reach over and touch her, to find a way to bridge the space between them. There was no way of knowing how she'd react, and so again, he left it.

What about your real brother, he said, do you know where he is?

I hope he is dead, she said. If he is not dead, he is still with the militia. And then he is better off dead.

It was months later that he invited her to his apartment. He want-ed to make her dinner, he said, but really he wanted to be in a safe place to attempt to touch her. He cooked steaks, the only thing he knew how to make, and put together a playlist of songs he thought she'd like. He bought wine, although he'd never seen her drink any, and cake for dessert, from the place they liked to go together. She was awkward and shy when she arrived. He offered to take her coat but she said she was cold. He made her tea to warm her up and still she looked like she would rather be anywhere else in the world than on his couch.

Shall we eat, he offered.

They ate mostly in silence, he could hear her chew and swallow.

My sister's having a baby, he said, she called today.

Dembe smiled stiffly, you will be an uncle, she said, that's nice.

He took another bite of steak. She finished her food and put her cutlery together. Was that okay? he asked.

Yes, she said. It was good.

He took the plates and put them in the sink.

Only, you look like you're having the worst time, he said.

She said nothing.

Do I make you nervous, he said. Do you think I'm going to hurt you, rape you, force you to do something you don't want to do?

He was almost shouting, he realized, and couldn't stop himself, because he'd done everything right and he'd waited and held back and still here she sat, terrified like stone, looking at him like he was a fucking savage about to pounce.

Here, he said, here.

He unbuttoned his jeans and pulled them down, pulled down his underpants and stood there, flesh in front of her, tiny pink cock shocked and exposed for her to see.

Look, he cried, look at me! I can't hurt you Dembe, he said, I can't do anything to you. He was standing there, sobbing and wretched and imagining what he must look like to her, what kind of revulsion his pitiful body would invoke in her as she looked upon his malformed flesh, his withered and shameful manhood.

She stood up from her chair and he imagined she would be leaving, out the door and never to be seen again. Instead, she walked to where he was standing, stood before him, looked him in the eyes and took his cheeks in her hand.

It's okay, she said. Do not cry, do not waste your tears.

She kissed him, on the mouth, tender but passionless, a matter of fact.

You will love me, she said, and I will love you back.

He took her hand and put it to his heart.

Yes, he said, that is exactly what we will do.

They lay together on top of the bed, her in her coat, him naked, and fell asleep. It was a deep, restful sleep, his hand touching her arm only lightly, afraid to leave too much of a mark.

In the morning, she was not gone.

WURDEN WIR MIT DEM LEBEN BELOHNT ODER BESTRAFT?

The man's a relic, a ghost from the past with skin so thin over bone you can see through it right into the veins and capillaries underneath, like the mechanism of a watch. He's far from home, far away as you can get, but since this is the only home he's known these past seventy or so years, he calls it by that name, *home*, and allows that in this case, like so many others, word and truth don't match one bit. It's okay, you do what you do to survive. That has always been the way, the constant in his life. Only problem, the question that's gnawed at him deep and sore most of his years, nagging, nudging: what's the point? it says and he knows the answer only too well.

You watch animals in the wild, the way they run from danger, hide, scamper up a tree or into a hole in the ground. Shaking with adrenaline, blood pumping to the brain, instincts in full force. *Survive, survive, survive* because that is what the living are wired to do. But sometimes the will to actually be alive in the world is nowhere near as strong as the will to simply survive. Life, so quick to be lost for some, is too firm in its grip for others. Look at him, a survivor of history and fate, living instead of dead, here instead of there, flesh instead of dust. He doesn't deserve it is what he thinks and he doesn't want it is what he knows for sure. But all there is to do is endure.

I have done terrible things. I have perpetrated great evil. Part of him wants to say the words out loud, wants to hear them hang in the air like a noose. Let me suffer, he thinks, let me pay. These words he says only in his head, but they're just as effective. Because this is his penance: life. Dull, inglorious, dismal life, eked out here in a seaside town on the tip of the African continent. Nowhereland, the only place he belongs.

He calls himself Benjamin. It's not the same name his mother gave him when she first put him to her breast, red and squirming and shocked at life, but that was another time, another life. He's no longer that boy and wishes often he never had been. It's strange, so much time in a place and still the accent won't dull unless he forces it to. Ditto the memories. He keeps waiting for the moment when his brain will start to deteriorate, when it all becomes a little hazy, a little easier to forget. But if anything, the past gets clearer every day, more vivid, more immediate. Perhaps it is the curse of old age, reversing time everywhere but in the body. Or perhaps in his case it's a curse of a different kind. A form of punishment, deserved and welcomed.

In the store he buys milk, buys bread, a little ham, a plastic tub of the cheaper butter. The girl at the counter smiles, always tries with him though she ought to have given up years ago.

Morning *Oom*, she says.

He hates it, the familiarity, the implied intimacy. *Oom*. Uncle. Benevolent stranger. He nods his head, he pays and mostly in coins so he can empty his wallet of the weight. The girl puts his groceries into a thin plastic bag that will likely split before he gets them to his kitchen counter. He's complained once before and she offered to sell him a bag made of recycled tires with a picture of a cheetah on it.

At home, he makes a sandwich, uses one slice of ham and leaves the rest for Minnie, who will come tomorrow to clean. He likes her, likes her more than anyone he's met here. That's saying a lot. It might be because she says almost nothing. Just cleans, dusts, takes the vacuum under the bed and around the living room. He senses that she wants to talk, that once she starts she'd never stop.

Stone Baby

They occupy the space in silence instead. Once, only once in the year that she's been with him has she asked him about his accent. Where's Master from? she said.

Again, a name that doesn't fit. But she can't bring herself to call him by anything else. History, handed down through the generations; sometimes it just refuses to let go and especially here where the before and after are often indistinguishable from each other. Europe, he'd answered, and she'd nodded.

I knew you sounded British, she said.

He only hired Minnie on the insistence of his physician, Dr. Mendel, who cares about the well-being of his patients in ways Benjamin can't quite fathom.

It was after a fall last year, Benjamin broke his collarbone and a rib. Dr. Mendel sat him down and looked sternly at him from across the desk.

You need help, he said. You're at an age now.

He gave him a number of a woman he knew.

Her name's Minnie, she's apparently very thorough, he said. A little slow but—here he held up his hands—she can do what you need her to do.

He called Minnie and she came round to his house the next day. She looked poor, slightly ragged, slightly wild. She picked at her hair and her hands as she spoke.

They sent me away from the farm where I lived before, she said.

Why is that? Benjamin asked.

She scowled. They say I'm gone crazy. *But hulle is mal.* She bit her lip and pulled at her fingers. *Die baba*, she said, they took the baby, killed him. I just wanted my revenge. Eye for an eye, like the Bible tells you. If it says it in the Bible it means God thinks it's fine. But on the farm they think they know more than God. She shook her head, wiped at her eyes.

He thought of a woman he'd met when he first arrived, a pearl-encrusted legal secretary who ran the bird-watchers' association.

The natives are rather colorful, she'd cautioned him at a party he'd been forced to attend. Best leave them to their dramas and not get oneself too involved.

She had tittered, touched his arm for a brief moment before he flinched and pulled it away.

Yes well, she continued. This is why things here work. Separation is sometimes the only way.

It sickened him somehow, the way things worked then. He had left one regime for another, and still he was on the winning end of the draw. They called him *baas*, master; deferred to him in simpering tones that brought too many memories to the surface. I am not your *baas*, he had said more than once.

The response was never relief, only confusion. Fear even. Eventually he stopped trying to resist.

Minnie rocked back and forth, nervous or mad. She said something else in Afrikaans and then stood up abruptly. She ran a finger through the thick dust on the bookshelf and said, Master needs a cleaner. I'll make it *lekker* clean every day. You'll see.

She came the next day and every day since. The house was spotless and in spite of himself he grew to enjoy the brief respite from solitude.

He goes into the bookstore every day, even Sundays. Some days it's just him, not a customer in sight, but still he sits, reading, waiting, lost in dust and yellowed pages. He bought the store so as not to arouse suspicion. He needed purpose, an income, however pitiful it may be. He specializes in rare editions, though these days there aren't many of them to be found or many people willing to pay for them. He loves being inside the store. The quiet, the smell. There aren't many people who step inside. A few locals, a handful of tourists. Few people buy anything, but it doesn't matter much. It is somewhere to go, somewhere not altogether unpleasant in which to spend the hours. A woman comes in, elegantly dressed, English accent, wellborn. She asks him for a copy of something by Deepak Chopra. He tells her it's not that kind of a bookstore.

Like clockwork, at six o'clock he puts on his hat, takes a walk to the beach to feel the sand underfoot and taste the sea on his tongue. He scours the shoreline for shells, bends with great effort to retrieve the ones he does find. He was an avid collector when he first arrived. He'd never before walked on the beach, felt sand between his toes or the bite of the sea breeze on his bare skin. The shells he collected then were beautiful, exotic treasures of the deep. Some days the shoreline was awash with color, delicate corals and giant queen conchs and urchins cracking underfoot. He remembered a book read to him as a child in which a young boy puts his ear to a shell and hears all the secrets of the world. He tried it once, strained for the sounds of a long-lost life, but there was only the dull echo of his own thoughts to be heard. He used to allow himself a single shell every visit to the beach. He'd find the one that he wanted, secret it into a pocket, and bring it home to place on his otherwise empty shelf. It was a small pleasure, minuscule in fact, but even so it made him feel like he was cheating.

There aren't so many shells anymore. The tides haven't changed over the years but what they wash up now is not the same as before. A few broken shells, mostly recently vacated mussels or periwinkles. Glass, plastic bottles, seals bloated and bitten or slicked in black oil. Once, a body, human and blue and only partially intact. A man, midforties. The papers identified him but not his killer, though they speculated it was a hit of some kind. He's watched the country change and shift, borne witness to the before and after. Everything once contained now is let loose, even here the town pulses with tension, violence waiting in the wings.

A woman walking her dog smiles at him and he nods in her direction. He considered a dog once, but decided against it. Living things, not his forte. Near the swings, a family is laying out a picnic blanket and unpacking food from a cooler. Mother, father, three children. They look like the cast of a TV commercial, smiling and shining. He winces.

The ghosts come to him mostly at night, in the darkness of his bedroom. They demand nothing of him, just an acknowledgment that they are there, that they once existed. Men and women and children, all of them ravaged by cruelty and inhumanity of the worst kind. Much of it inflicted by him. They watch him watching them. They know everything but they say nothing, which might be worse. He would like them to scream, punch his chest, hold his throat till the air has nowhere to go, in or out. Sometimes the ghosts are on the television too, in the newspapers or in magazine articles, though less so as time passes. Still, the stories never seem to end. Tales of unspeakable horrors, heroes and villains. An inexhaustible supply of facts, even now with so few witnesses still alive to speak of it. Never forget, never forget. He would like to say things to them, *I'm sorry. I did not want to be there. I did only what I was told.* But words in this context have no meaning and no weight, they vanish into the air like breath, unseen and unfelt to all but him.

It was Andreas who suggested it. The only way, he'd said. Run or die.

The rumors of the end of the war were flying around the camp, everything falling apart. They fled in the dead of night, two men, coats and boots and a pitiful crust of bread apiece. First thing they did was find a barn. They crouched down, one held a torch while the other cut. Blunt knife in flesh; it was a massacre in the straw. Benjamin vomited.

Pull yourself together, Andreas said. You've seen worse and done worse.

He took the knife and finished cutting the SS tattoo out from under his arm.

Now your chest, Andreas said. It has to look like a bullet went through. Afterward, the two men stitched the flaps of skin while the discarded parts of themselves wept into the dirt.

Auf Wiedersehen, Führer, Andreas said.

He laughed. Benjamin wondered how.

They walked for many days and nights, passing one ruined village after the next. Occasionally a peasant woman spat at them; they could not help but look like soldiers. The pain from the wound was excruciating.

Andreas sniffed under his arm. Gangrene, he said.

They sat again with the knives and dug the infection from the wound. Andreas poured whiskey from his flask onto the open flesh and screamed.

Better to die at our own hand than in some fucking prison, right, he said.

When they neared the Dutch border the two men parted ways.

Andreas shook his hand. Good luck, he said. From this moment we are new men.

He had no trace of anything resembling remorse or fear.

Where will you go? Benjamin asked, suddenly anxious at being left alone.

Andreas shrugged. I will think of something.

He walked at night, creeping through the dark like some feral beast, ravenous and full of terror. During the day he slept in abandoned sheds and existed on almost nothing, roots, grass, beetles. How had they done it, how had any of them managed to survive the camps on what they fed them? He felt the shame wash over him, nauseating and heavy like lead. Already he could feel his rib cage, count the bones. It's good if you look like you have been starved, Andreas had said, but there was little choice in the matter.

One night in a small cabin he'd come upon in the woods, he woke to find a man standing over him.

You are running too? he asked in German, Bavarian by the sounds of it.

Benjamin nodded.

The man sat down, removed his boots, and breathed into his hands to warm them against the chill.

I am Mank, he said. Commander Mank. At least, that is what I was until two days ago. Now, he said, now I am a fugitive.

He laughed bitterly, shook his head. We were gods and now we will be dogs, scavengers like the rest of them.

Benjamin said nothing, afraid to speak, afraid not to.

Are you proud of your actions? Mank asked. Have you served your country well, obeyed orders, served the Führer?

Benjamin said quietly, I do not know if I served my country, but I obeyed orders.

Mank narrowed his eyes. He went quiet for a few minutes before he spoke again. Do you know, I have everything I need to start a new life. Money, papers, contacts. I will be a free man. Without history, without consequences.

Yes, Benjamin nodded, this is very fortunate.

Fortunate! Mank snorted. He took a drink from a flask and passed it to Benjamin. No, my friend, he said. It is not fortunate. It is an injustice of the worst kind.

In the morning Mank was blue and cold, hanging from a beam by his belt. Benjamin cut him down and the corpse fell on top of him, pinning him down. He lay still for a minute, the weight of the dead man crushing the air out of his lungs. Was this the way it was meant to end? he wondered. He closed his eyes, weary, surrendering. There was a noise and he started. Fight or flight. There was no other option. He pushed Mank off him, reached into his coat pockets, and found a wad of notes, a pile of jewelry, a list of names, a passport. He looked at the name, at the photograph. Benjamin, he said aloud, trying it out. I am Benjamin. He took a long drink from the dead man's flask, slipped out of the barn, and kept going until he reached the Cape of Good Hope. Along the way he used the bills, doled them out to the names on the list. Men looked at him without judgment. They knew, of course they knew, but still they helped him, pointed him in the right direction and toward the right people. He handed them payment, money or gold, which they slipped indifferently into their jacket pockets. They said nothing, not good luck, not good riddance.

In Cape Town, people welcomed him, took his word for who he

was and where he was from. The accent he explained was Swiss, the reason for choosing South Africa on account of his father's upbringing in Namibia. Return to the roots and such, he mumbled, and they nodded, yes, yes, they understood. Still, in the city he felt a little exposed; after some weeks he decamped to Kalk Bay, occupied then only by fishermen and the odd retirement home. For his first few months he rented a room in the home of an elderly widow who was as eager to talk as he was to be silent. Her husband had been a missionary, doing God's work she told him with shining eyes. Later she told him about the young girl he had impregnated and run off with.

Black as the ace of spades, she said, and it was clear this was the greater outrage of the scandal.

In town, he would find himself surrounded by middle-aged women. You must meet my daughter, they would coo, hopeful that this beguiling foreigner might sprinkle their lives with a little glamour. He was always polite but curt, soon his reputation was established. Aloof, they warned newcomers, keeps himself to himself. Some of the less-forgiving women spread rumors, not entirely untrue. Because even before, when it might have been possible, he never quite took to the idea of women in the way young men are supposed to do. He had contemplated it only once, the fact that he might be bent in an entirely different way. The idea terrified him, he never dared entertain it, let alone act upon it. His father would have disinherited him, killed him even. And afterward, as a soldier, well, he saw enough of those kind heaped in piles, the undesirables.

When he found a cottage of his own he paid for it in cash and moved in the next week. The widow visited him with a casserole some weeks later. He had nowhere for her to sit and she did not come back. The house was sparse, cold, bordering on uncomfortable. Alone once again, he felt the silence envelop him. Solitude. Loneliness. An absence of warmth. Yes, he wanted it just so. To feel burdened by life. To feel anything but spared. At first he imagined this life might be temporary, a way to hide out for a time until he felt ready to rejoin the world. But the years snake up on one another, they gather in volume until the years already spent are too numerous and the years remaining too few. In the end, he stayed, just here, just this life. Him and the ghosts, mirror images of one another; neither cruel nor kind, just there to hold up a reflection.

It must have been around twenty years after he had arrived. A man came into the shop with his wife in tow. His accent was a mix of America and the distant past, the old country of his birth and despair. Benjamin always recognized accents that were half-hidden, he knew the effort it took to keep them unrevealed and could pick up the words that so unkindly betrayed their speaker's true heritage. He looked into the man's eyes and a flicker of recognition hit him in the gut like a bullet. It had to be him. The mouth, the color of his eyes. The way he carried himself on unsteady feet, not yet accustomed to freedom and possibly never to be. He was frozen, could not open his mouth to speak even when the man asked him a question. Do you have this or that, he was inquiring, but all Benjamin heard was his heart pounding in his chest and the history flooding back, unstoppable in its force.

The man had been a boy of twelve, maybe more, maybe less. It was so hard to tell when they were that emaciated and well shorn. You could hardly tell the men from the women. Benjamin was responsible for clearing bodies from the showers. He enlisted several prisoners for the job, each one instructed to load a wheelbarrow and then transport the newly dead to a large pit. Their reward was an extra piece of bread, sometimes a potato, half-rotten but better than nothing. Solemn and gaunt, the men worked, barely alive themselves but still with enough fight in them to do whatever it took for food. Idiots, one of the other officers had remarked, don't they know they will be dead soon regardless.

The boy was one of them. He approached Benjamin one morning when one of the regular prisoners keeled over dead in the snow, from disease or exhaustion, no one knew or cared.

I will do it, the boy said. Pick me. I am young and strong and faster than the rest of them. Pick me, he insisted.

He had looked at his frail form and old-man eyes, not a hint of child left in him. He agreed to let him work. He stood near the boy and watched him, making sure he did things according to the regulations.

At one point the boy pointed to a body and said, this is my mother.

Later he pointed again. This is my father, he said.

He was calm, matter-of-fact. Maybe he had already cried out all his tears. Or maybe he was too young to recall a world where humanity had existed at all. His face, his eyes, Benjamin had never forgotten them.

In the shop, he stared, fixated, waiting for the moment when memory would kick in for the younger man, waiting for him to step back, horrified, fully revealed.

It's you, he would say. He would tell his wife, the whole town would gather. They would cart him off, an old man with hardly any hair and a stoop in his gait. Murderer. War criminal. He would be tried and hanged, and justice would be served at last. But the man showed no signs of recognition, none at all. This was just another man, another face before him. He left the shop with a leather-bound edition of *Crime and Punishment*. Thanks for your trouble, he said cheerily on his way out, his wife echoing his words with a thick American drawl.

Benjamin, trembling, sank into the chair behind the desk. The thing he felt, it was disappointment.

In the years since and the ones that came before, he has spent much time thinking about Mank, trying to make sense of the man's suicide, trying to understand his own life in relation to it. Was it shame that killed him or the fear of living the rest of his days inglorious and anonymous? Was it a test of his own morality, his willingness to be complicit in the injustice of escape?

He will never know. What he does know is the number of times he has considered following suit, ending this dull and unbeloved existence that serves no one and least of all himself. He would not be missed; it might even go entirely unnoticed. In his lower moments he even contemplates how he might achieve his end, preferring something bloodless and clean. Now of course there is Minnie to consider. She would be the one to find his body. He would not wish to upset her. In the end, it is not this that stops him, but fear. Not of death, the finality of the end, but of not living out this sentence; this self-imposed but necessary exile from the world. Of course it is ridiculous, a contradiction in terms, but he will feel that he is cheating if he does not continue to live on, barely and begrudgingly, each day the same as the one before. Empty. Alone. Penitent. If there is to be no punishment, at least there will be this.

Partly, he believes that there must be something to it, a higher power seeing to it that his years are long and his pleasures few. He is ninety-six years old. Alive longer than anyone ought to be, really, and especially someone like him. But there are no signs of an end being near, no signs of illness or a lurking murky death. He has aches and pains in his joints, and a mild cough from smoking his pipe. But apart from that, nothing. He checks himself frequently in the macabre but always thwarted hope that something may reveal itself. But the moles do not grow, the lumps fail to appear. His organs conspire against him, keeping him well. People he knew when he moved here are dead, cancer or heart mostly. Sometimes there will be a comment in passing from a surviving spouse. You must have longevity in the genes, they say mournfully. Meaning: how is it you are not yet dead? He doesn't know if it is genetic or not. His parents he never saw again, there was no way of knowing the lives they led after the war. He imagines his father might have concluded things much like Mank. Perhaps a bullet to the head in his study, his war medals pinned to his jacket.

The sun is setting, almost violent in color. Breathtaking. There are tourists posing in front of their phones, capturing memories, keeping time. The woman walking her dog has finished one length of the beach and is making her way back. She smiles at him again. He dusts the sand off his feet and puts his worn shoes back on. His toes are gnarled with arthritis and he notices that his nails need to be clipped again. It is work he dreads, since these days the undignified struggle to bend over far enough quite winds him. He has considered asking for Minnie's help, but always rules against it. The idea of being touched is surely worse than the discomfort of bending over.

He has decided that he will leave the cottage to Minnie when he does at last die. He has written it in his will. There is no one else. Besides, she is a woman who has suffered more than her share of life's cruelties. He would like to feel that he is bestowing a small kindness on her. He likes to imagine her face when she hears the news. A house? For me? She would put pictures of her boy on the walls, the dead baby. Maybe hang curtains or line the stark walls with wallpaper. Grow flowers in the beds out front. She would make it a home, transform his cottage into something that could sustain life. She likes to dust his shell collection. She would keep those, maybe hold one to her ear every now and then and remember him fondly. A man who had given her a gift. A man who had done some good. It was ridiculous, he knew. He cleared the thoughts from his mind but left her name in his will nonetheless.

At home, he sits awhile, staring at the walls around him that have done so fine a job of keeping the world out. He's too tired to read, too bored of the television to switch it on. He nods at the ghosts in the room watching him in silence. Does he imagine it or is the look they give him pitying? He brushes his teeth, splashes cold water on his face. The man in the mirror looks back at him, nods knowingly. It's the same every night. He climbs slowly into his bed, the sheets newly washed and smelling of the detergent Minnie makes him buy. He breathes a heavy sigh. He is weary, a dull pain nags at his side, his joints groan. Perhaps, he thinks, perhaps tonight. He closes his eyes and hopes, as he does each night, not to open them in the morning.

LOOK AT WHAT YOU'VE DONE

Conor Walsh will you look what you've done. These are the words of my mother's that I remember most clearly. Maybe because she said them so often. Maybe because even now, I look around and there are so many reasons she might say them to me. For example, standing among the organic root vegetables at the grocery store, picking sweet potatoes for the soup I now know how to make by heart and finding the living ghost of Grant's mother, Diane, in front of me. She looked at me like she thought she knew me but wasn't quite sure. There may even have been a window of opportunity where I could have pretended not to recognize her at all, but then we locked eyes and I suppose it came flooding back.

Conor, she said, as I live and breathe, Conor Walsh is that really you?

Right then I didn't want it to be, not one bit, but I put on my best smile and said, Hello Mrs. Sullivan, how are things?

She couldn't take her eyes off me, looked me up and down and inside out. Her eyes watered as she took it all in.

Jaysus Conor, she said, you're looking well.

She didn't look overly happy about that fact, and to be fair I could understand why she wouldn't be.

I was sorry to hear about your mum, she said, she was a lovely woman, she really was.

I nodded, stomach lurched. Not what I wanted to be discussing in the vegetable aisle, if anywhere. She kept staring at me, searching, for clues or evidence perhaps.

You look so well, she said again, almost in a whisper. Real healthy like, she added.

Her eyes fell down to check my arms, all clear, all clean. I read the surprise written on her face and felt the guilt shoot through me like it usually does when confronted with people from the past.

How is Grant getting on? I asked, because not to ask would be admitting that I already knew what I knew.

Mrs. Sullivan narrowed her eyes at me and shook her head. Well, she said, it is what it is, I suppose.

I looked into her cart and saw six bags of crisps, a few bottles of cola, and three packs of Hicks sausages. Maybe she was having a party. I noticed her face was ancient, lines cutting deep across it to demarcate every tragedy the years had sent her. It reminded me of the way my mother looked, even years before the cancer came to finish her off. Hurt writes itself on the body in one way or another, marking time, making sure you don't forget.

Mrs. Sullivan, I said, I should go. Please send Grant my regards, and—and you take care now.

She didn't move. Oh Conor, she said. Remember how you lads used to play together as kids? Building forts in the back garden all summer long.

Yes, I said, sure I remember, and I do.

She took me by the hand suddenly, gripped firm, cut into me with her rings. Please come by and see him, she said. Please.

Her eyes were wide, her voice shaking. Every part of me wanted to say no, scream it actually, but instead I heard myself saying grand, yeah, of course I will. And in the great scheme of things I suppose I owed them at least that much. A couple hours of my time. A small penance for all that they have endured.

We agreed to Sunday, we agreed to sometime after lunch. Her face leaked gratitude and tears; she was overcome. I leaned over, pity or remorse or maybe some kind of longing for my own mother kicking in, gave her a kiss on the cheek. She laughed nervously, stepped back. We Irish not being built to carry quite so much emotion.

What am I like, she said, crying like a baby in the bleedin' supermarket?

I wanted to give her a tissue or something but all I had on me was an old handkerchief stuffed into my pocket from when I'd had a cold last week. She wiped at her eyes with her sleeve instead.

I'm so happy to see you like this, Conor, she said again, I really am.

At home, Fee was fresh out of the shower, hair wet and feet dripping little puddles onto the tiles. Fee, my fairy Fee. She kissed me, and I put my hand to her belly where the baby we made felt hard against my palm. You could trace over the bones of the fingers and the toes, the ridges of the spine as the baby turned and curled like a cat. Life, forming right here before our eyes. I am terrified. Of deformity and disease, that my past will catch up to me in the form of defective sperm and a mutant child. Divine retribution for all that I have done. I've told this to Fee, because I tell her everything, and she stroked my face and hushed me.

Your aura is a beautiful one, she said. Everything in balance, the darkness gone. She kissed my eyelids and the end of my nose. Fairy Fee, savior of man.

She works as a Reiki practitioner and a yoga teacher. She says she can feel a person's energy from afar and I've never told her otherwise. She was in a car accident when she was sixteen where she lost an eye and gained a scar that cuts her neck in two. I kiss the markings of her flesh the way she kisses the scars I wear on the inside, with tenderness and love, as though they were sacred markings. In her spare time, Fee makes jewelry using crystal and semiprecious stones. She made me a bracelet of quartz, good for healing energy, also a deflector of radiation. I wear it every day without fail, if only because it makes her smile. Fee is exactly the kind of woman I used to despise in my other life. In this life, she is everything that matters; an anchor to the world of the living and the good.

We unpacked the groceries together, Fee still in her towel, handing me things to put away.

Did you hear any word from Laura? I asked.

Laura is Fee's sister, currently backpacking with her friend Xanthe through India but out of touch for the last couple of days.

No, Fee said, and her face darkened briefly. I don't want to say something's wrong, she said, but energetically, it just feels kind of cloudy at the moment, and with the storms on the news . . . She shook her head. I mean, it could just be because Mercury's in retrograde, is all.

I agreed, I nodded; I knew all about Mercury and its positioning these days. I moved behind Fee to cup her breasts and kiss her neck. She smelled of lemons.

I love you, I said, because I say it daily.

Here, she said, and put my hand to her belly so I could feel as the baby kicked.

If it's a girl, we plan to call her Iris, after my mother. If she were alive, my mother would have pretended to be embarrassed by this level of reverence, but secretly I know it would please her.

I bumped into Diane at the supermarket, I said.

Fee made a face, like a grimace. That must have been hard, she said. How is Grant?

I shrugged. I told Diane I'd visit him on Sunday, go round to the house. I couldn't really say no when she asked, I said.

Fee bit her lip, opened her mouth, and then closed it again. Listen, she said, it's not your fault. Their situation. You know that, right? You're only responsible for your own actions, no one else's. And you were kids. Just kids. No one could hold you accountable. She kissed my cheek and went to get dressed.

I know, I called after her, you're right.

But that was a lie.

I look back on those years wishing there was something more concrete to make sense of it all. The how, the why. They were such a nice family, weren't they, the gossipmongers at church would say, all the while licking their lips for more juicy details. No, maybe that's unfair, maybe they felt the weight of sadness and loss, maybe they really did keep us lost souls in their prayers like they vowed to do each week. Or maybe they just thanked the sweet Lord that it was anyone's kids but their own. I don't know why I started using, what I wanted to achieve or obliterate. Nobody fiddled with me as a boy, nobody made me feel unloved or smothered by love. I wasn't some outcast or rebel. I was just me, dumb-as-fuck kid trying to act bolder than I felt. Bored, probably a little depressed, maybe even lonely in the way of all teenage boys lost in their awkward selves. I really can't say. All I know is that I took them with me, Grant and Lissa, tangled them up in my stupidity until they had no way out. I ruined their lives. Yes, I did. I can say it because it's the truth, one of those irrefutable facts that cannot be rewritten, no matter how many organic vegetables I consume or how sparkling a state I get my aura into.

Conor, Grant, and Lissa, our little holy trinity of destruction. Lissa, in love with me, Grant trying to pretend he didn't feel the same, and me lapping it all up, oblivious to the consequences. Free will is a beautiful concept but it has no place in teenage love triangles. I didn't want to be alone in what I was doing. Grant and Lissa didn't want to be without me. So we went down together. I bought the first pills from money I'd saved making fake student ID cards on my computer at home. We went to Phoenix Park like we did most Friday nights back then, a mass of kids with all the cans we'd managed to beg, borrow, or steal. I remember taking Lissa and Grant a little away from the others, showing them in my hand what I had procured.

Now lads, I said, we can get langers like always, or we can try some of Dublin's finest. Grant had looked worried. Jaysus, I don't know Conor, he said, that's not messing about. And me, Conor Walsh, so full of certainty about life and the future and everything in between, I turned to the boy I'd grown up with like a brother and said, will you ever stop being such a mammy's boy, Sullivan?

While our classmates drank until they worked up the courage to snog someone or vomited onto their shoes, the three of us took three little pills and put them on our tongues. It was like it was supposed to be, almost spiritual. Lissa lifted off her shirt and let me run my hands under her bra while Grant lay rolling on the grass. We held hands and danced to the music coming from one of the cars and everyone looked at us knowingly and a little afraid. We felt edgy and special, different at last, and the night was long and beautiful and even the next day when our heads hurt and we sweated through our clothes we knew it wasn't going to be the last time.

There was a lad in his first year at Trinity who sold stuff between lessons. We'd meet outside the off-license and make an exchange like we were gangsters in a movie. I still think that was one of my favorite parts. At school we managed to concentrate enough to pass our final exams, but all we were interested in was the next score and the next big night. The other kids in our year looked at us with something between contempt and respect; or at least that's how we saw it then. They don't have the balls, we'd say, but really they might just have known better. My parents, they didn't suspect a thing, looked upon me adoringly and brought me cups of tea when I lay in bed shivering and sick to the stomach.

I didn't get into any of the good colleges, none of us did with our leaving cert results, but we shipped off to Limerick and enrolled in fairly useless English and arts degrees. Our digs were positively postapocalyptic, a mess of bottles and pizza boxes and guitars. We were happy as pigs in shit. In our first few weeks, Lissa's dad, Harry, visited us on his way back from a business trip. He looked around, picked a piece of ham off the wall from where someone must have smeared it in a drunken state. He took us to Johnny Rockets for Smoke House Doubles and shakes and dropped us back to the door afterward. Lissa kissed his cheek and he drove away, never to return even though he passed through at least once a month.

The substances we were on at that time were varied and expensive. We hit our parents for bigger allowances and subsidized the rest with odd jobs here and there. We felt then like a tribe, hanging out, living together, looking after one another. In truth, we didn't much worry about anyone or anything besides our own fixes, although those days weren't even the worst of them. If I think back, I can see Grant, blurry-eyed and growing thinner by the week, pale even for an Irishman. Still he looked at me with those eyes, pleading, hopeful. A dog just waiting to be petted and I would indulge him from time to time, when it suited me or when he was feeling generous with his stash. He might have tried to kiss me once, I may even have let him. Lissa and I, we drifted away and back toward each other like moths above a flame, dependent and drowning. She would sleep with me most nights and with others when she was in the mood for meanness. There was a dealer she sometimes went home with; when she'd walk in the next morning she always looked the worse for wear but too high to register it.

It sounds like those years were a haze, but there was a sharpness too, an aliveness we felt and chased and never managed to hold on to for any length of time. Still, there was a sense of normalness to our days too, attempts to study, parties at the digs, dates with other students, visits home to Dublin on the bus. We managed to pull off most of what we needed to do, if only just.

At some point, maybe it was our final year, Lissa said she was quitting. She'd been home to Dublin for her grandmother's birthday and had run into one of the girls from school.

She was so together, she complained to us afterward, so feckin' self-righteous with her career and her car and her Brown Thomas shopping bags.

Grant and I were confused. Are you jealous? we asked.

She stormed out of the room and a day later made the announcement to us. She moved out some weeks later and after we graduated we didn't see each other for years. I'd hear things through mutual friends, that she was clean and then that she'd been busted for selling. I think a part of me was glad she wasn't doing any better than us. I still don't know why.

Grant and I lived together after college, spent some years working dead-end jobs and trying to keep our parents fooled. We played PlayStation through the night, smoked or snorted or shot up what we could get our hands on. I dated some girls, Grant got serious with a culchie from Kerry, farm-raised and in for the shock of her life when she realized six months down the line that her fella was a drug addict. Catriona was her name, Catriona McCabe. It was her that called up Grant's mother, told her what was going on. Diane came right over, pounded on the door till we opened up in our shorts, pupils dilated from the night before, apartment a massacre. She was sobbing, heaving.

You fools, she screeched, you feckin' morons, getting yourselves involved with this drugs business.

Grant broke down in tears, said over and over, I'm sorry Ma, I'm so sorry.

I don't remember much of what happened next, but there were meetings with my parents and the priest and a psychologist, and then the two of us handed in notice at work and sublet the apartment and got hauled back home to be under our mothers' noses once again.

There were some good years and some bad years that came after that, never one or the other for long. I watched my parents recoil from me, one too many calls from the Garda, one too many mornings waking up to find the house ransacked. My mother aged, my father drank. I took responsibility for none of it, just came and went and let them pick up the pieces when things fell apart. There were many low points, one of the worst being an afternoon shooting up on the pavement in Cook Street, looking up and seeing my father, hand over his mouth, unable to contain the horror.

You're dead to me, son, he said.

He'd been out shopping for my Christmas present. I wasn't allowed back in the house, my mother told me with tears streaming down her lined face.

We just can't do this anymore, she wept, it's killing us.

I floated between homes, bumming a few nights on the couch with friends who hadn't yet cut me off, or staying with Diane when she'd have me. Grant continued to live with her, she wouldn't kick him out or cut him off. She'd raised him alone, him and his older brother, guarded those boys like a bear and refused to give up. At some point, my parents stopped speaking to her too, they thought she was enabling our addictions. My mother called me from time to time. We met for lunch occasionally, always somewhere dingy where there'd be no risk of running into anyone she knew. She'd give me money, kiss my cheek, and try not to cry.

You know you only have to say the words and you can come home, she'd always say at the end.

I didn't say the words until last year, thirty-three years old. My Jesus Year. I looked a decade older, some teeth gone, my face gray and lined, everything a mess. I had a job waiting tables in Temple Bar, serving tourists pizzas and penne arrabbiata. I was sleeping on a mattress on the floor, sharing a place with two twenty-year-olds and a middle-aged Polish builder. I hadn't spoken to my father in seven years, had heard from my aunt that my mother was sick, and left it so many months before I worked up the guts to see her that she died in between. Grant I knew was back home after a bout living rough and an arrest for solicitation. Someone told me he was messed up this time, messed up for good, but I didn't know what it meant and didn't care to find out. Then one day, there she was on the news. Lissa, once-beautiful Lissa, being led in chains to a police van. Half a kilo of heroin, she was lucky to escape the firing squad, but there she was, other side of the world, game over, life in ruins. And I saw it all, our lives played back in slow motion like a movie montage. *Conor Walsh, will you look at what you've done.*

Fee and I ate lunch at the table and I watched as the mother of my unborn child took small bites, each chewed sixteen times until swallowing.

Still no kale in the stores? she asked.

I shook my head, nope, no zucchini either.

Jaysus, she said, at this rate we mightn't be far off from another bloody potato famine.

I ate my salad and wished for a cheeseburger. I thought about the visit to Grant, the ways I might get out of it or the things I might say to him if I couldn't. Hey, man! Looking good. Long time. How're tricks? What do you say, what are the words you're meant to find? Fee asked me something and I realized I hadn't been listening to her. She got up from the table and went softly into the bedroom.

I'm not pissed, she called, I'm just sensing that you need time in your own head.

I went into the spare room—the baby's room—and sat staring at the pile of boxes. I was meant to be sorting through them, making space. Fee's already hung a multicrystalled mobile on the ceiling that will help balance our child's chakras from an early age. The crib is my old one, retrieved from my parents' garage and given a lick of paint by my father. We are tentatively finding our way back to each other, him and I, though his trust in my new life is fragile at best. As it should be, I suppose, given everything that has come before. Given the fact that I too feel like an imposter in this shiny new-fashioned life I find myself living. I am forcing myself to belong, to brunch at Avoca on Sundays and plan winter sun getaways to Tenerife, to talk about grouting and O'Driscoll's retirement from the rugby like these are weighty matters of great concern. It's like a game of pretend, only my mother doesn't call me in at the end of the day to remind me of who I really am.

The boxes, they're a time capsule. After my mother died, my father tossed them out onto the street, left a message on my phone telling me to collect them. It was the one thing my mother would never agree to do. She always kept my bedroom exactly the way I had left it as a boy, maybe hoping to return to that moment and start it over. It must have been cathartic then for my father to go through with it at last, erasing the son who had sent his wife to an early grave and filled his life with nothing but one disappointment after the next. When I collected the boxes, I caught a glimpse of him in the window, watching me cart my life off his lawn. I think I wished he would run out and stop me, or punch me. We haven't yet discussed my mother's death, and perhaps we never will.

I opened the first box, pulled out old posters, a photo album my mother made of me as a baby, the train set my grandfather had hand carved from wood. History, my history, everything preserved and contained; an archive of lost years. Cassette tapes, Metallica T-shirts reeking of sweat and dust, a pile of photographs. One of them was of me and Grant, hamming it up for the camera. The Before Years. We must have been thirteen, fresh-faced, on the cusp of our unraveling. He was a beautiful boy, in the way of most lost boys who are beautiful and young for only a brief moment before life chews them up and spits them out. I remember the day the photograph was taken. It was after school, we were hanging out at Grant's house as we mostly did back then. Diane had made us grilled cheese and onion sandwiches, served with a side of King crisps. We were lying on the couch, watching a rerun of *Back to the Future*, speculating about which of the inventions might be possible in our own lifetimes. Diane came in with the camera and told us to smile.

Come on lads, she'd said, let's immortalize you two hooligans.

How did it happen, that moment to this? I thought of Grant, of Diane in the supermarket. My stomach lurched. I took the photograph and put it into an envelope.

Sunday came and a wave of dread washed over me. I didn't know what to wear, how to look respectable but not too prosperous. I didn't know if Grant was expecting me to be my old self and I didn't know how to be my new self with him. I brought Fee a ginger tea and kissed her good-bye.

Good luck, she said, remember your center.

I decided to walk, went along the canal past the swans and their day-old baguettes, past the stragglers making their way home after a night out. There was an overturned buggy in the water, half-drowned and wheels up. I wondered where the baby was.

Outside Diane's house I took in a breath. The place looked just the same as before. I rang the bell and the door opened. Diane was smiling wide, full of faux cheer.

Well Grant, she said, look who it is!

She ushered me into the living room, where Grant was sitting on the couch.

Go on in, Diane said, I'll bring you boys something to drink.

It was strange to be referred to as boys, stranger still to be back in the house like no time had passed at all.

Jaysus, Mary, and Joseph, will you look at what the cat dragged in! Grant said.

He laughed and slapped at his knee. I smiled wide, put out my hand, tried hard to still my heart.

How are you, Buddy? I said.

It was a shock to the system, him in the flesh; grotesque and misshapen, a caricature of who he once was. Morbidly obese, wedged into the couch by a sea of flesh, his face was twice the size of mine, bloated like one of those corpses found in an advanced state of gaseous decomposition. Beautiful Grant, heart of gold, soul of a poet.

He looked me up and down, taking in the years, the damage.

You look good, he said, a little sullen. Real good.

Ah you know, I said, the girlfriend's one of those health nuts, got me on all sorts of regimens, yoga, superfoods.

I stopped talking because I sounded like an asshole, but he nodded his head, apparently approving. I wondered whether or not to tell him about the baby, decided against it. It would sound too much like bragging.

I'm a mess, aren't I? he said. Fat as fuck, balding, sweating like a pig!

He said it almost proudly, like it was some kind of an improvement on what he was before. Maybe it was. The last time I'd seen him was more than two years ago, we were in the park, off our heads. His eyes were bloodshot, his body skeletal, skin hanging from him like a cloak. Did I ever tell you I wanted to be a vet, he'd said, horses and cows in the country, that's my feckin' wet dream. We'd laughed, the idea of dreams and futures absurd.

He was sweating profusely, his face clammy and red. There was a fan on the table and a towel beside him that he used to wipe his neck, and every so often under his breasts, which were large and swollen like a woman's. He lifted his T-shirt, revealing an enormous gut, pale and hairless like a baby. He caught me staring and shrugged.

What can you do, he said, my metabolism is shot to hell.

Ah, I said, the important thing is that you're clean.

Jesus, I was making myself cringe.

Grant laughed, would you listen to Betty Fucken Ford over here! he said. Ah sure, you're right, though. Guess it's a good thing I fucked myself senseless through my twenties, you'd need a map to find my cock these days!

I noticed that he was overtly camp now, no longer ambiguous with his gestures and his tone. He took the towel and wiped his neck again. He smelled strongly of sweat and decay.

Jaysus Walshie, he said, you look like someone died.

I tried to laugh but it came out more like a squeal. I looked at the front door longingly.

So, what are you doing with yourself these days? I said, for something to say.

I pretty much knew the answer already. Grant looked at me like he'd never really thought about it before.

I guess I stay in a lot, he said. Watch a lot of movies, bit of the old Xbox. Don't go out much anymore, the sweats you know, anxiety, and what have you. I can't really take a job or do a lot of stuff, I guess. Plus, he said, pointing to his head, things are a little fried, you know.

He laughed, too loudly. Anyway, he said, it's pretty sweet, this setup, like. Not much more you could ask for, right?

He smiled at me, the smile of his sixteen-year-old self, and you could see that he was stuck, just there, forever suspended in that moment. A child in the body of an oversized man.

Diane came back in with lemonade and a bowl of crisps.

Cheers, Ma, Grant said, and she gave his head a little pat.

You sweet boy, she said, you dear sweet boy.

When she'd left the room he put a handful of crisps into his mouth. Did you hear about Lissa? he asked.

I nodded, yeah, I said. Pretty awful, twenty years in prison.

I didn't tell him it had been the turning point for me, maybe the thing that had saved my life.

I reckon she masterminded it, Grant said, that Lissa was always a feckin' wild one.

Her da's there now, I said. He up and left.

Grant cackled suddenly. Old Harry! Remember his face that time he came round to our digs?

I took a sip of the lemonade, unsure of what to say, aware only of his chewing and his breathing, both of which sounded like a struggle.

You still going big, partying hard? he asked me.

I shook my head. Nah man, I said, it was time to stop, time to get out before it destroyed me.

I said the words and instantly wanted to take them back, but Grant took no offense.

That's a shame, he said, those were good times. Best years of my life, I reckon. He looked suddenly wounded and I felt the guilt of all the years past and all the ones still to come, heavy and helpless in the pit of my gut.

Mammy's boy. I gave his arm a little punch, trying to be playful, trying to find a way back.

Damn right, I said brightly, because it was all I had left to give him. They were the best years for sure, Buddy.

His face lit up, that smile again, wide and oblivious.

Yeah, he said, fuck yeah.

Diane padded into the room, this time with a dish of cookies.

He gets low blood sugar if he doesn't eat regularly, she said.

Grant handed me a cookie and I ate one, catching the crumbs with my other hand. Diane stood a while hovering over us.

Isn't this marvelous, Grant, she said, you and Walshie together again?

Grant looked over at me and winked. To be sure it is, Ma, to be sure it is.

I looked at my watch, imagined Fee curled up on the couch with her book. I longed to join her, to breathe in her smell and be swallowed up by her goodness. Grant grabbed the remote and started flicking through the channels.

Wanna watch something? he asked.

Diane looked over at me, held my gaze with those eyes that begged and pleaded.

Sure, I said, absolutely, but I want to show you something first.

I reached into my pocket and took out the photograph, handed it to Grant, who held it up for Diane to see. She smiled, a mix of grief and joy, put a hand to her heart.

Yes, she said, I remember that day well.

I settled back beside Grant on the couch, gave him a nudge in the ribs, which he returned. We laughed and were boys again.

It was after midnight when I left.

Will you come again? Diane asked.

I kissed her on the cheek and she didn't flinch.

Every week, I said.

She had already found a frame for the photograph and set it on the mantelpiece. Two smiling boys, the future at their feet.

TELL ME SOMETHING NO ONE ELSE KNOWS

It's weird that I'm telling you this, isn't it? I mean, I know it's what we agreed: a secret for a secret, but still. I've told no one else; in all likelihood I probably never will. Just you. You and me, random and fated at the same time.

Do you think perhaps we were meant to meet? I hope so. I hope in fifty years' time we look back on this night—this wild and strange and otherworldly night in an airport in the middle of India—and I hope we say, damn, that was something, wasn't it?

It's funny, you think you can live with all sorts of secrets, private burdens that wake you at night with a start, but the truth is, I suppose we all long to confess our sins, to find some sense of absolution in the face of whatever terrible thing we've done. I guess our secrets are a little different—yours about your mother more than you. You're guilty only by association, because you know that she hired someone to kill your father. You didn't do the deed yourself, you didn't even know about it until afterward. There's a part of me that even admires her—oh, don't be angry—I know it was your father, but you have to give her credit for how she planned it all to look like a break-in. In the end, it sounds like a crime of love, like all she was trying to do was put him out of his misery. It's not much consolation, of course not, but at least it was free of malice. Mine was not.

I can't really start anywhere but at the beginning, so perhaps it's a good thing we're stuck here all night. I don't even mind airports,

I like the constant flow of people, coming and going, finding their way home or taking themselves as far away from it as they can get.

Anyhow. I left for my trip to Asia imagining that it would be somehow life changing—as these trips tend to be. My parents encouraged me, said it would be good for me. My father once traveled through Africa in a Land Rover, crossing overland from Botswana and all the way up to Algeria. He said it was the best thing he ever did in his life. I wanted that too, some big and bold adventure that would define me, perhaps give my life something solid to anchor itself to. I don't know what I was looking for exactly. To find myself, I suppose, that most wretched of clichés. It's cringeworthy, isn't it? That whole *namaste, namaste* spiritual tourism crap, the hordes of lost Westerners looking for redemption and meaning in places with cold showers and weak currencies. Well, I was one of them.

I didn't plan on Laura coming along. I didn't really want her there in the first place. We were in touch, always had been since I moved to Germany. We had a weekly Skype date, Tuesday evenings, eight P.M. We'd be lying in our beds, cups of tea in hand and laptops balanced on a pillow on our thighs. I always checked my hair first in the mirror before we spoke. I told her what I had planned and her eyes went wide; I don't think she imagined I had the guts for something like that. Alone? she kept asking, and I said yes, just me and a backpack. It made me feel fierce and impressive, like the kind of woman I always admired and despised at the same time. How can you afford it? she asked and I lied and said I had some really big commissions for work. She always called me the Princess, and I hated to prove her right. But there's another confession for you: I'm a trust-fund kid, just as spoiled and indulged as you'd imagine.

It was maybe two or so weeks later when Laura texted me. BIG NEWS, she said, CALL ASAP. I'm coming along! she shouted into the phone when I rang her. She'd already bought her ticket, sublet her place in Dublin, taken a sabbatical from work.

I just couldn't let you go alone, she said.

My heart was pounding, inside a voice screaming, NO. Because this was meant to be about me, just me. I think I said something unenthusiastic or maybe even a little bitchy. I remember Laura sounded wounded.

Oh, she said, I thought you'd be pleased.

I said I was pleased, just surprised. I may or may not have told her that I originally wanted to be alone, that the trip was meant to be a kind of soul-searching solo mission. It wouldn't have made much difference either way. Laura always heard only what she wanted to hear.

We both flew to Frankfurt and took the flight together from there. We hugged when we saw each other and I was struck like always by how beautiful she was. Even tired and red-eyed, even with her hair messed and her skin oily, she had a glow about her. Men always stared, women too. It's just because I'm smiley, she used to say, knowing full well it wasn't. Her sister had made us matching agate necklaces with a little note enclosed. *Agate harmonizes yin and yang, the positive and negative forces that hold the universe in place. It brings balance, calm, and truth. Safe and happy travels to the goddesses Xanthe & Laura xxx.*

She's a total hippie, right? Laura said, but we tied the necklaces around our necks all the same. We held hands as the plane left the runway and toasted to our travels with tomato juice and salted almonds.

We arrived in Delhi to chaos and craziness, another world altogether, as you know. My head was spinning from the heat and the jet lag, we took a taxi to our hostel and nearly died seven times over on the way. No lanes, no lights, just horns honking and a constant death-defying stream of cars. I wanted to feel excited and I was for the most part, because wasn't this what it was all about—the great unknown, this parallel universe of existence across the sea? Laura was laughing and joking with the driver, already at ease. She was always a chameleon, she could fit herself to any situation she was in. Another thing I envied about her. At the hostel, we checked in at the front desk and left our bags in the room. It stank of sweat and dirt, the covers on the bed looked like they'd never been washed and the wiring for the electricity hung precariously off the walls and buzzed when you walked underneath.

We're a long way from home, Dorothy, I said and Laura clicked her shoes together.

It was this thing we did.

I needed to use the toilet and almost vomited when I did. The stench, the floor streaked with shit and piss and blood. I squatted over a hole in the ground and then realized there was no paper. I passed my hand under me and pulled up my jeans. Welcome to India, I thought.

We'd been warned of course of Delhi belly, but Laura decided that our first meal should be street food. We walked through the markets, teeming with people and smells and garbage; everywhere we went men grabbed at our arms and tried to sell us things. The heat was sticky and close, my shirt clung to my skin, which already had a layer of dirt and sand coating it. The pollution was suffocating, it was difficult to breathe. All around, buildings were collapsing or in the process of being built. The ground was covered in mud and puddles, piss or rainwater or both. Beggars without limbs and eyes, bandaged and bloodied, held out their hands and pleaded for money or food.

Isn't this amazing? Laura said, and I agreed, enthusiastic as I could muster.

We found a queue of people gathered around a vendor and lined up for our lunch. We watched the man deep-fry something in an old petrol barrel heated over a fire, we ate with oil dripping down our chins and tears streaming out from our eyes. It was spicy and hot and sat heavy in our stomachs. We climbed the stairs of a rickety bar and drank beers on the terrace, overlooking the sprawl of life below. It was nothing like I imagined, nothing at all.

It looks like the end of the world, I said.

Isn't that the point? Laura replied.

She was sick soon after, violent vomiting and diarrhea. We ran back to the hostel so she could use the bathroom. I brought her water and tied back her hair and wiped her face with the corner of a towel while she purged her insides of the lunch. The woman who ran the hostel handed me a mop and a bucket and told me that we'd need to clean up the mess. Laura stayed in bed for three days, weak and sweating out the sickness. I didn't leave her side, even though she told me I ought to.

We only have a few days here, she said, you should see the city.

I gave her a glass of water with electrolytes and hushed her, I'm not leaving you like this, I said.

The truth was I didn't want to leave. The room was vile but at least it offered some respite from the city outside, from the assault on the senses that waited for us below. Also: I liked the fact that Laura had fallen ill and I had not. It felt like I was ahead.

When she'd recovered, Laura and I took a bus to Agra to make our way to the Taj Mahal. It was on my bucket list, a wonder of the world and all. Laura wasn't that eager to see it, she'd already decided it was going to be a tourist trap, and I guess it was in the end. We were sold a camel ride and a personal guide, both pretty useless. But the site itself does take your breath away. It is quite magnificent. And naturally, a love story above all else, a testament to grief and loss. I liked that part the most. All around us there were couples kissing or posing for pictures; a mecca for love. They all seemed so sure of themselves, so confident that their pilgrimage would cement their love, make it as permanent as the marble and the stone.

We returned to Delhi late that night after another terrifying bus journey. At some point the driver swerved into oncoming traffic; it appeared he was almost asleep. He pulled to the side of the road and poured a bottle of water over his head. An old woman sitting across from us said something in French, a curse I think. From Delhi we headed to Jaipur, the Pink City, with its crumbling quarters and once-grand palaces. We stayed in a hostel that overlooked a busy street. The noise was deafening, the smog from the motorcycles and tuk-tuks choked you every time you ventured out. I developed a cough that wouldn't stop; after two weeks I think I must have cracked a rib. It was agony. Laura and I fell into some kind of a daily routine, starting with breakfast bought from the side of the road, usually fruit or anything we could find that wasn't covered in a layer of dust. We'd wander the streets, browsing the markets and annoying the vendors when we failed to buy what they were selling. We watched the women, veiled in swathes of cloth, and marveled at their bellies, fat and fleshy and protruding proudly from beneath their saris. The men laughed at us and blew kisses as we passed them by. We bought scarves to cover ourselves but still they looked at our bare legs like we were meat in the window of a butcher's shop.

Most days we'd take in some of the sights from the guidebook—the Hawa Mahal, the palaces, the observatory—and spend the rest of the day in one of the tourist restaurants with free Wi-Fi and half-decent Western food. At night we'd find a bar to sit at, drinking cheap happy hour cocktails and waiting to be picked up. I know, not exactly a whirlwind adventure, but the things you seem to go in search of when you're away from home tend to be the things that remind you of it. Still, it was a buzz. Being so far away, being so free. It made us bold. We took boys back to our hostel or went home with them to theirs. We had a little game between us that we called flags, the objective of which was to sleep with men of as many nationalities as we could. I think after Jaipur I was in the lead with seven. Not something to be proud of, but there you have it. One of the flags belonged to an American. He called himself Wolf, although I doubt that was his real name. He bought us daiquiris and sat between us at the bar, the meat in the sandwich, he said. Laura asked what kind of meat he imagined he was, and he said, Wagyu beef, baby, which made us all laugh.

He was flirting hard, the two of us batting our lashes and leading him on. Of course he was fixated on Laura, but I suppose he thought it wouldn't hurt to get two for the price of one. At some point Laura and I looked at each other and made the signal, which meant we were game. We'd talked about it once before, figured India was as good a place as any to be a little outrageous. When the bar closed, we invited Wolf back to our hostel, snuck him in through the garden, and made him promise to be quiet. Wolf stood there in the dim light and kissed us, first me and then Laura. As he pulled back, Laura said, I think I'll leave you to it.

She picked up her pack of cigarettes and gave me a wink as she closed the door behind her. You should have seen Wolf's face, it crumpled like a child whose ice cream's just fallen off the cone and onto the floor. I must have said something snide, because he started kissing me, trying to make up for it. But the moment had already been lost. There was no denying the fact that I was the dud consolation prize. We made our way through awful sex. I don't even think he finished. When he left, I went outside to find Laura, who was sitting in the moonlight smoking. She lifted her brows when she saw me.

Laura, I said, what the fuck?

She looked incredulous, like it was me who had it all wrong. Jesus, she said, I just thought I'd let you have all the fun to yourself.

That was so typical of her, to do something deliberately malicious and then act like it was some kind of grand gesture, some benevolence on her part. There was no point trying to argue; I went to the room and got into bed in a huff. When we saw Wolf later that week at the bar, he ignored us completely.

It was around that time I received some news from a gallery in Berlin. I'd been invited to participate in a group show, my very first exhibition. Oh, you know the kind, one of those generic Berlin galleries that hosts obscure artists and their often dismal work. People only come to the opening night for the free wine or if they happen to be one of the artists on show, but still it was everything I needed to feel like my life wasn't totally pointless. I read the e-mail and screamed. We were in the common area in the hostel, and Laura came over to see what I was reading.

Oh, she said, that's nice for you.

Nice. That was the best she could do. Later, she introduced me to people as "the artist," always using her fingers to make quotation marks in the air.

I'm so proud of you, she said, I really am.

It wasn't the first time with Laura that she'd done that, managed to take something good and sour it for me. She had that side to her, she relished it. I know all female friendships have a degree of jealousy and competitiveness to them, that it's normal for friends to be wary of one another's triumphs. Such is the downfall of feminism, right? But no, the thing with Laura went beyond that. It was something else.

Yes, I envied her beauty, her confidence; I envied the way she managed to make it all seem so easy, whatever life threw at her, she seemed to come out on top.

But something lurked in her, a darkness. I'd always been a little afraid of it. I'd known her since we were six years old, we knew each other inside out, down to the inner workings. Perhaps we knew too much. Other people, they liked her instantly, she drew them in like a magnet. She had that broken-winged-bird fragility, those doe eyes that watered at the drop of a hat. She lost her parents when she was young, there was that to make you feel for her, and it worked a treat with the men she met. They love a girl without a daddy, she always said. See, that's what I mean—she had a self-awareness to her, like she knew how to play every game there was. And our friendship was definitely a game. I'm trying to explain things properly here, to give it all a context. Still, I suspect it all comes across as being childish and petty and silly. Well, perhaps it was some of the time. And I'm aware that there are always two sides to a story, with the truth lurking somewhere in between.

We left Jaipur after a few weeks, took a bus to Udaipur to complete the Golden Triangle. After that, we were planning to head to Goa, for sea and sun and the yoga retreats that we'd booked from home. I was looking forward to getting away from the cities, the hordes of people all pulling at you constantly for something or other. Laura had sunk into a kind of fug by then too, she looked bored most of the time and didn't want to see any of the sights we'd earmarked for Udaipur in the guide. You go ahead, she'd say, and I would. It was a relief, those hours away from her; I felt like I expanded with every breath. Someone had warned me before I left that one's best friends often make the worst travel companions. It was true, Laura and I were horribly out of synch. We became catty and biting, every interaction an opportunity to wound. It's a terrifying thing, how quickly you can evolve into someone you don't want to be. I'd get back to the room after a day of sightseeing and she'd be lying there sprawled on the bed, Pringles cans and Snickers bars around her, watching movies on her iPad. The resentment I felt was palpable, and the same could surely be said for her.

We'd make plans for the day and she'd decide just before we left the room that she wanted to do something else instead. At night, she'd shower and change and go out on her own, not a word to me about where she was going or an offer for me to join. But the strange thing was, I didn't mind one bit. It dawned on me that I was having a much better time without her. I was enjoying myself more and more, feeling confident on my own, happy to explore the city and chat to strangers. Yes, alone I was the person I wanted to be; with Laura I was reduced always to the meager sidekick. I started going out at night too, heading to bars I assumed Laura would avoid. Udaipur was full of people to meet, waifs and strays and dreadlocked backpackers who'd arrived and never left. I fashioned myself into a real extrovert, friendly and chatty and fun (everything I'd never managed to do in Berlin, although it was the point of me moving there in the first place). I drank, smoked, got stoned; the nights were long and warm, they drew you in and held you close. I met people from all over the world, teachers from Spain and writers from Iceland and doctors from Argentina. I stopped noticing the stench and chaos of the city below, where the elephants and cows and motorbikes shared the streets with piles of garbage and too many broken souls to count. I stopped feeling irritated by the cold showers and the squat toilets, by the pace of service and the constant harassment of the locals. Everything was beautiful and I felt alive. This was the trip I was meant to be having. Me, on my own, like I'd planned it. I thought about ways I might suggest to Laura that we continue separately, but I couldn't see how she would take it well.

Then one night we did end up at the same bar. I'd come back to the hostel just as she was leaving. I noticed that she was wearing my shirt but never said anything. At the bar, I spotted her with a group of guys, three or four of them all hanging on her every word, waiting to be the one she picked. I was sitting with a group of Canadian backpackers who'd invited me to travel on with them as they made their way south. They were really nice, down-to-earth, the kind of people who were easy to hang out with. Anyway, sometime later, I looked up and Laura was standing there with her drink in her hand. The guys she had been with must have left, because she was clearly alone.

Well look who it is, she said, really friendly and chipper for a change.

I was a little drunk, a little tired of her behavior, and so I gave her a really withering look and said, do you need something?

She looked at me and her face fell. She shook her head and walked away and I turned to the others to continue the conversation. It was cruel, I know, but sometimes you had to do that with Laura, remind her that she wasn't the center of the universe.

She didn't come home that night, or the next two after that, and suddenly I began to feel real panic that something terrible had happened. When she finally walked through the door, I jumped up and gave her a hug.

I was so worried, I said.

She disentangled herself from my arms and looked at me, surprised.

I didn't think you'd care, she said, you seemed pretty happy with your new friends.

I burst into tears, maybe from the relief or the buildup of all the weeks we'd spent together, making each other miserable. I'm sorry, La, I said, I don't know what's happening here with us.

Pretty hostile, right? she said.

I nodded and we hugged and apologized and made promises about starting over and getting into our travel groove. I held her tight and felt her breath on my neck like a whisper. I loved her, you know, like a sister.

Over the next few days, we had a blast, just the two of us. We hung out on the hostel terrace reading our books, and took long walks around the old town, stopping for lassis and pancakes and treating ourselves to some new dresses for Goa. At night, we'd lie in bed watching movies together, her head on my shoulder, my arm around hers.

This is nice, she said, and I agreed.

That was the thing with us, we always came back to each other in the end.

We walked past a tattoo parlor one afternoon, soon after we arrived in Goa.

Oh, let's, Laura said, and so we went inside.

It was a skinny New Zealander doing the tattoos, he had dreadlocks and a bolt through his nose.

What do you have in mind? he asked, and of course we didn't have a clue.

We looked through the magazines in the shop for about an hour and then Laura threw her hands up. What are we like, she said, it's so obvious!

I knew instantly what she meant—when we were little girls learning Irish in school, we'd discovered the Celtic symbol for sisters. We spent a full year drawing them on our wrists each day, just under our watch straps. Sisters forever, we said. We had the tattoos done one by one, Laura first while I watched and wished for a way to get out of it. She'd never have forgiven me if I didn't go through with it, so I gritted my teeth and looked away while the New Zealander marked forever the flesh around my ankle.

God, I just realized I've told you our real names, I wasn't even thinking. But—it doesn't matter, does it? I know you have no interest in using this for anything other than a way to pass the time. You'll catch your flight back to South Africa, and I'll take mine to Dublin. You'll start your new job on that wine farm—as a viticulturist, was it?—and I imagine this will soon be nothing more than a distant memory, a faded snapshot of a night that was, with a girl you'll never meet again. There's a certain poetry to it, don't you think? Two marooned souls, two airport confessions with nowhere to go but here.

Old patterns are hard to break. It's the basal ganglia, you see, the part of the brain responsible for habits. The neurons, they remember everything, even when you try to change, the memory of the old pattern will always be stronger. Laura and I, we lasted a week or two with our little truce, but sure enough, little by little things reverted to the way they were before. There were scraps over boys and clothes, we couldn't spend more than an hour together without a fight. I laughed one day at the pair of us.

We're like an old married couple, you and I, I said, full of nothing but spite and resentment.

I longed to be on my own, to be that self I was when Laura was out of the way. I'm sure she felt the same—only she never would have said. Perhaps only to punish me.

I used to watch a lot of crime shows on TV—you know the ones. The case always boils down to a crime of passion or a premeditated crime, even though neither makes a difference to the person who's dead. What I did, what I did in the end to Laura, I guess you'd have to call it a crime of passion. Love and hate, they're two sides of the same coin after all and I don't suppose you can explain it any other way.

I guess up north where you were traveling, you had more of a warning about the storms. Down south where we were, we didn't see much news and there wasn't really any talk of the weather. We were staying in a youth hostel off the main street—about a five-minute bike ride to the beach. Laura had been down the hall taking a shower when the manager came to the door. His English wasn't very good, but he managed well enough to make himself understood.

Storm, he told me, maybe tsunami.

He made a gesture with his hand, curved it like a wave over his head. No beach today, he said, no swim.

Yes, I said, I understand.

Laura came back into the room in her towel and pulled on her bikini. Her body was taut, firm from all the walking and brown from all the sun. Look at me: skin so pale I'm translucent and a body that will never be anything but a mushy and tragic pear.

I'm doing my own thing today, she said.

I shrugged, okay, I said, no problem.

She glared at me. Well you don't have to sound so happy about it, she said, it's not my fault this dynamic is so fucking unstimulating.

I might have said something then, or maybe I just let her be. In any case, she finished dressing and locked up her backpack. Outside, the sky was milky blue, a strange glow creeping in.

Where are you going? I asked.

The beach, Laura said, hopefully I'll find some company that's a little more interesting.

I looked at Laura, that smirk, that way she had of relishing the wounds she inflicted. My friend, my lifelong friend. My longtime nemesis.

Laura, I said, and that was the moment—that split second where I could have said what I ought to have said. *Laura, don't go, Laura, there's a tsunami coming, Laura, please stay here and be safe. Laura, Laura,* you made it so easy not to.

She hung back in the doorway and raised her eyebrows at me. Yes? she said.

Oh, nothing, I replied. Have fun.

There are many ways to pull a trigger, the outcome is the same. I didn't imagine that she would swim into the sea and emerge from it a corpse, bloated and recognizable only for the tattoo on her ankle. I don't know what I thought, what I hoped would or would not happen to her on the beach in the face of that tsunami. I don't think I wanted her dead, no—most certainly not—I don't even imagine I wanted her injured. What I wanted was to be absolved of the burden, the burden of Laura. That was all. I think that was all.

I heard the screams, the chaos as the first waves hit and the village scattered. It was bigger than they had predicted, the damage far worse. It lasts so briefly—you must know from your own experience—but the aftermath is in slow motion, a montage of the worst scenes you've ever seen. I knew as I followed the crowd down to the beach to survey the damage that Laura would be gone. There was no way to survive something of that force. I felt a strange mix of numbness and terror—that moment, it had changed everything, and there was no going back. A stranger took my hand and I sobbed and sobbed.

It's okay, he said, you are safe now.

At the hostel, they were already clearing branches and debris.

Where's your friend? the manager asked, and I held my hand over my mouth so the screams would not get out.

Days later, I worked up the courage to call my parents. The tsunami wasn't even news—too few casualties and too many other crises to report on.

What about Laura, my mother asked, she's okay?

She's missing, I whispered into the phone.

The body took some days to wash ashore. A fisherman hauled her out of the water and a man from the Irish embassy flew in to help with the arrangements. I spoke to Laura's sister on the phone, tried to make sense of what she was saying between her tears.

I'm so glad her last days were with you, she said, you were her other sister, Xanthe.

I can tell myself that I didn't force her into the water, that I cannot be held accountable for acts of God, as they declare such things on insurance forms. I can tell myself that it was not malice, and only the omission of a few words, that ultimately it was Laura's own free will that led her into the sea that day. I can tell myself all sorts of things, and none of them will be true. None of them will make me anything other than guilty. Because Laura being dead, that's on me. It's been two weeks now, that's how long it's taken for everything to be arranged. We'll be flying home together, the two of us, me in a first-class seat—can you imagine, they've upgraded me because of my ordeal—and Laura in a box in the hold. It's possible it might have been the other way around, that Laura might have been the one to send me unknowingly into the belly of the beast. I like to think so anyway. I like to imagine that our friendship was somehow destined to be fatal. Maybe Laura will even have the last laugh after all. I feel her, the nights I wake in a sweat from a terrible nightmare, only to discover that there is no dream to wake from. Those nights when my heart is in my throat and my throat is constricting like there's a hand wrapped around it, twisting, choking. That's Laura, that's her reminding me that she's still on top.

This is life, isn't it? A series of moments that build into a lifetime. Moments that define you without you even realizing it. Indelible, never to be undone. That moment, that will be forever who I am, no matter what else I do or become. The knot of malformed sisterhood, written into my soul.

Well, there it is. All I have to tell. You must hate me, or think me the worst person in the world. It doesn't matter, I suppose. I think we're being called to board, I ought to go. I—I hope you have a happy life. I hope it unfolds how you wish, and when it does, you like what you see. I hope you find a way to forgive your mother. She will surely never forgive herself.

BUILD, BREAK

The house he was building took up three plots. He'd bought the first house and decided it was too small. The neighbors he paid off, wrote out checks for double the value of their properties. They were elderly, had lived in the same homes all their lives, raised up children and grandchildren on those immaculately mowed lawns. Games of tennis, summer cocktail parties; most of the children had married in the garden, the guests seated at long white tables under the shade of the ancient oak. Still, they moved quickly, most likely into gated communities where the security was tight and the neighbors kin. On the same day they left, he had the demolition team arrive to blast the houses to the ground. He'd watched as they detonated them one by one. Boom, blast, the bricks and cement and heavy wooden beams collapsing in on the houses they had once held up. Progress, he'd thought. Sometimes it's building something up, sometimes it's tearing it down.

Alain the architect exclaimed in his thick French accent, you are the Genghis Khan of Bishop's Court!

He did not know if it was a compliment or an insult, but he smiled anyway. What did it matter. He was here. He owned the land. He could do as he wished.

This is illegal, screeched the woman from across the street. You're a fucking criminal, a fucking monster!

The houses were meant to be protected property, historical monuments that had stood for more than a century, rooted to the land like trees; impermeable, immovable. They were the homes of founding fathers, the men who'd built the country. And some of the ones who'd broken it too. The houses were thick with the grandeur of another era, immense dining halls and book-lined libraries and kitchens with that little row of servant bells still clinging to the walls, a bell for each maid. Another time, another world. He had no reverence for such homes. They were not his history, and he wanted them gone. A clean slate, a new beginning. *This is how it is now.*

He had a friend at the local council, a young man who called himself Shakes and was not difficult to pay off. He checked the cash in the envelope and slipped it into his coat pocket.

Nice, huh? he said, stroking the material. Armani. So, he continued, something like this—it's not that difficult to pull off. You get the demolition guys to tear the houses down first, then you apologize. *Oops, sorry* baas, *I did not know.* The houses are gone, flattened! They can do nothing but shake their heads at the sorry state of our once-great nation.

The two men had laughed, clinked their glasses together and enjoyed the slow heat of whiskey as it moved down their throats. They'd been sitting at the bar of the best hotel in the city, drinking the barman's finest Scotch.

Two fingers for an arm and a leg, he quipped.

He'd never much liked the taste of whiskey, but had cultivated an appreciation for it over the years. Along with other things that marked this life from the one that had come before.

Next to them, there was a table of young women out celebrating a hens' night. All of them blonde, tanned, squeezed into too-bright too-tight dresses. Shakes sent over a bottle of champagne and at the end of the evening took the maid of honor home in his sports car.

Man, she was a fucking wild thing, he reported the next time they spoke.

Progress. Change. The new world order.

He visited the site every day. His land. His dream house. He didn't want to miss a thing. The foreman loathed him, he could tell. Spoke to him in the way most people did, a mix of disdain and deference.

The team of builders watched him like hawks, eyes darting up and down, taking it all in. Black man, black Porsche, building the biggest house that had ever stood in the whitest suburb in the city. He liked how they looked at him, how they'd have to speculate about how he'd made his money. *Baas*, black diamond, coconut.

He didn't care what they called him, cared only that he wasn't one of them. Poor, desperate, living hand to mouth. Everything about him, suit, swagger, everything screamed *look at me, look at how I am nothing like you.*

A self-made man. He loved that term. A man who makes himself. His first deal, he'd signed in fifteen minutes, before the coffee had even cooled. *Er, yes Mr. Sisiwe, we think you're just the partner we're looking for.*

Bunch of old white men, gathered around trying to slice up the pie. He'd looked at their faces, the ties they wore, the shoes on their feet, the gold watches handed down from fathers on their deathbeds. Money, old and entrenched. But look at them now.

Cowering before him, calling him mister instead of boy. Part of him pitied them. Forced to fill affirmative action quotas, forced to put a few token dark faces on the board. Still, he hated them more than he pitied them, hated what they stood for and what they'd gotten away with. He told them what he wanted, watched them shift in their seats, looking nervously around for an alternative.

Yes, well, that is a very large percentage, they muttered.

Yes, well, I am a very black man, he replied.

They shook hands and he left; the start of everything that was to come. Make them pay, make them sorry; maybe that was what he thought back then. Now, it was only about the money. He read his bank statements every day, checked the zeros to see that they were all there. Millions. A millionaire. Him. It made him smile, put a spring in his step.

He had an office, more for show than anything else, but he went in most days regardless. He liked the smell of the leather chairs and the whir of the coffee machine, he liked the papers that were brought to him to sign and the young colored receptionist at the front desk. He'd fucked her a few times, found it mildly memorable. Every day she wore the necklace he'd bought her, touched it with her fingers as he walked past each morning.

Mr. Sisiwe, she always said, trying to maintain some air of professionalism.

She had a child, a boy of three who'd sat watching an Afrikaans soap opera on the TV in the kitchen while his mother undressed for her boss in the room next door. Her underwear had been cheap and frayed, it had embarrassed him on her behalf and although at the time he'd made a mental note to replace it for her, he never did.

He took the elevator to the top floor, used the time to look at his reflection in the mirrors. Sharp was what he was going for, expensive suit, Italian shoes, heavy gold watch.

Lately, he'd taken to collecting watches; he'd read somewhere that Jay Z had more than thirty. He worked out every day with a personal trainer, drank protein shakes and pressed juices. Look the part, the rest will follow. He checked his teeth, white, gleaming against his skin.

You're the color of money, his cousin Mo liked to say.

They'd grown up together, peas in a pod. Now Mo was a preacher in the township, asked sometimes for donations. For the kids, he said, but he drove a red BMW and had a girlfriend who was seventeen and rumored to be pregnant with his child.

In his office, Athene the interior designer showed him options for chandeliers. She smelled of French perfume and wore her blonde hair in a severe bob that didn't come cheap. She wore tailored suits and large gold earrings that looked like they strained her ears. He'd brought her out from London, on the recommendation of an acquaintance who had homes around the world. She's the best, he'd said, and that was all that he needed to know. She'd asked for a budget at their first meeting, but he'd only laughed.

As you wish, sir, she'd said in her accent, thick with empire and privilege.

By now she knew what he wanted. Imported marble, chandeliers out of French châteaux, classical statues. He'd heard her one day on the phone, talking to a supplier.

Yes, I want it in gold, she'd said. He's building a fucking Xanadu.

Bigger, better, shinier. He wanted it ostentatious, offensive to the sensibilities of his neighbors, outrageous to his own friends. He wanted it to groan with wealth and excess; he welcomed ridicule and scorn. Let them see, let them know. Let there be no doubt at all.

His wife was embarrassed. It's too much, she said.

No, he replied. Nothing is too much.

He liked handing the invoices over to his secretary, he liked to watch the way her eyes scanned the numbers, trying and failing to be subtle. A hundred thousand for a bathtub? You fucking bet. She was white, in her fifties. Her husband had been retrenched five years ago from his job at the bank and still had no work. Some mornings he overheard her on the phone, trying to sound encouraging. He saw in the parking garage that her car had changed from an Audi to an old Toyota, said nothing but felt strangely pleased about the turning of their luck. He'd noticed her maiden name on the job application form, one of those last names laden with too much history and shame, a marker of guilt. Maybe that's why he hired her above the others, to make her bear witness. *Look, see, understand the new rules.* The hatred he felt toward her was potent, just how he liked it. It fueled him, always had. In her eyes, barely concealed beneath politeness and efficiency, there was hate to match his own. Loathing, repulsion. Would sir like a coffee? Can I order sir some lunch?

He imagined the stories she would report back to her friends, to the husband at home. The way she would refer to him in private, the word she might use. It delighted him. Hate me, he thought, hate me so much it hurts.

You've changed, his wife told him some years ago, eyes bleary from tears that appeared more and more frequently.

She had grown up in the home of a white family, her mother was their live-in maid. She inherited the children's old clothes and toys, and at Christmas there was always a gift for her under the tree. She'd had her schooling paid for, she never went hungry. It was a luckier childhood than most; sometimes they teased her at school because of her accent and her fancy clothes. The things he loved about her when they met were the things now that made her seem overly provincial to him.

I don't recognize you, she told him, you are not the man I married.

But she was wrong. He had not changed, it was the world around them that was different, making new things possible. He kept a photograph of his grandfather in his drawer. He had been photographed in the forties by Cronin for his book *The Bantu Tribes of South Africa*. Awkwardly perched on a stool in a studio, spear in hand, a novelty to be paraded around the world. *Uncircumcised boy*, the caption read, with nothing more to give him a name or a place in the world. And now, well, now Athene was presenting him with outrageously expensive prints by contemporary African artists who photographed white people in tribal costumes.

This artist, she'd said, he's from Zimbabwe. Very hot market right now.

He'd picked out the four prints that he disliked the least and Athene nodded, great choice, yeah, she said, such great commentary on colonial othering and exoticism.

Sure, he agreed, sure.

At his son Zed's school, a black child was made head prefect, the first in its long history. He cared, but not greatly. The photographs of the sports teams that lined the corridors, they were a perfect chronicle of the country's transformation, a slow and small shift of power. How the old boys struggled at the school's centenary celebrations, having to shake hands with all the new blood, the moneyed elite who didn't care much for the traditions that the others held so dear.

Zed didn't want to play soccer, he wanted to play rugby, a white man's game. He took a lithe blonde called Misty to his winter dance, hired a limo to pick her up that he charged to his father's credit card. At the front door, her parents shook his hand, said nice to meet you with wide smiles that didn't move. Progress, change. This was where the real transformation could be seen, not in the townships but in the suburbs, in the gradual infiltration of neighborhoods and schools.

You know, he'd said at a party once, most white people feel safer having black criminals in their streets than black neighbors next door!

Everyone roared with laughter, particularly the white folks who liked to show they had a sense of humor about themselves. They were the worst, trying so earnestly to flaunt their progressiveness.

We're here because we love this country, they said, we want to make a difference, be part of the change.

Some of them showed him pictures of their adopted children, dark and smiling in bonnets.

Sure, he said, smiling, nodding, knowing the reason they stayed was because nothing had changed for them. They had more to complain about, more to fear perhaps, but they just closed the bubble tighter around themselves, keeping in what they wanted, keeping out the rest. Easy enough to do if you could afford it, which plenty of them could.

At the traffic lights, children in rags came to his window and put out a hand. Please, they said, eyes milky from disease or sniffing glue.

He shook his head. Nothing for you today, he said, to himself really, because the window was rolled up.

Didn't move him, the plight of his people, because he didn't think of them as his people. His people were the ones like him, made over shiny and new, taking what was theirs.

You've arrived, my man. He said it to himself every morning. Splash of cologne, watch on his wrist, sip of espresso from the coffee machine that cost more than his first car. The sheen of money was unmistakable. He walked into the finest restaurants and they'd call him by name, bring over wine from the cellar. Perhaps sir would like to try the cabernet? Yes, sir fucking would. He made money and spent it. Wined and dined politicians and business-men, received invitations to their holiday homes in France and to sundowners on their yachts. He said yes to everything, smiled the smile, talked the talk. Flew first-class to Dubai every few months to entertain a Saudi billionaire who hated black men but liked to fuck the women from time to time. He brought them over as assis-tants and handed them to Saeed like a bottle of wine from a din-ner guest. In return, deals agreed, contracts signed, money made. Sometimes his photograph would appear in the gossip magazines, some hot young thing draped over his arm. He loved it, kept the articles in the bottom drawer of his desk and looked at them from time to time. Money. Notoriety. These were the achievements that mattered now. Even some of the politicians understood it, posted pictures online of their flash cars and custom-made shoes. Strug-gle? Struggle is over, brother.

The transformation of the property was slow, held up by strikes and power outages. He wanted to be in by Christmas, had plans for a New Year's party.

When will we be ready, he asked Alain.

The Frenchman had smiled. My previous project was in Doha. There, the men work twenty-four-hour shifts. It is never a day late. But here . . . he laughed. Here, one day is a taxi war, the next day a steel strike. The men break for lunch and do not come back. You do things differently over here. Africa time, they call it, yes?

I'm in a hurry, he said, pay them double.

Alain pouted, yes, of course, he said. You can pay them double and they will still do half the work.

The woman from across the road watched him from her balcony, looking down at the gaping hole in the ground where homes had once stood.

It's disgusting what you've done, she called. Fucking disgusting. You people have no respect!

You people. It almost made him smile. He waved at her, to be ironic or perhaps insulting. From afar he found her mildly attractive, if a little skinny for his tastes. She gave him the finger and retreated inside behind the curtain. Alain raised his eyebrows. You do not make many friends, he remarked.

The neighbors to the left of the property had come over to introduce themselves when the builders first broke ground. Sally and Roman. They'd stepped over the rubble and the dirt, smiled wide, tried to appear nonchalant.

Welcome, they said brightly. Welcome to the neighborhood.

They smiled at him, he smiled back, just a couple of friendly faces in the suburbs. He tried to picture neighborly barbecues, him and Roman turning steaks on the flames while the women gossiped and prepared salads. Maybe. Maybe not.

So what are your plans with the place? they asked him.

Sally had brought over a loaf of banana bread from the deli, wrapped in brown paper and string to look suitably artisanal.

He told them the plans, watched their eyes grow wide.

Shit, fantastic, brilliant, Roman said. About bloody time we saw some new faces around here.

Sally gave him a look, like he'd said something idiotic, ruined their spiel. They wished him luck with the builders and turned to leave.

Sally called over her shoulder, we'll do dinner, just as soon as you're all moved in.

Oh, looking forward, he replied, a parody of himself.

Now the first level was nearing completion and Sally and Roman had left. New Zealand, he'd heard.

The landscaper called him to the site one day, a problem, she'd said over the phone. Her name was Esme, had skin like a boot from too many years spent squinting into the sun. She wore men's combat trousers and an old Habitat for Humanity T-shirt.

So, she said, these plans for the pool. They didn't take into account the roots of the oak.

She held up plans, marked with a pencil an alternative place for the pool. Look, she said, if we just move it to here, the guys can work around the roots without harming the tree. She spoke with a thick Afrikaans accent, hard vowels and rolled *r*'s.

He looked briefly at the plans and then at her. I'm not moving the pool, he said.

She gave a little laugh. But this tree is probably two hundred years old, she said, I mean, at the very least. You can't just chop down a two-hundred-year-old oak tree.

Alain hovered, watching. He gave a little wave of his hand. Of course we can move the pool, he said, there is space enough to put it on the other side, off the main terrace. The access will be just as good.

He glanced at Esme, who nodded. They'd already discussed it without him.

No, he said. Let's take the tree down. I want the pool to stay as planned.

Esme bit her lip, shook her head. She turned to look at Alain, who lifted his arms and shrugged. Esme shook her head, said something in Afrikaans under her breath.

Alain touched a hand to the oak. She is very beautiful, he said, wistful.

Esme quit the following week, maybe because she could not stand taking orders from a black man, maybe because the plight of the tree was just too much to bear. Another landscaper was hired, paid, instructed to remove the tree. He stood and watched as men took blades to the branches and the trunk, and the tree fell in pieces to the ground. The scream of the saws, the thud of the logs, an entire afternoon it took to take down the great oak. When the roots came out, they lay splayed beside the tremendous void in the ground like the bones of a carcass, naked and exposed. Athene was there that day, trying to make calls above the noise.

I want two of these logs, she shouted, nice solid rounds. We'll make coffee tables for the terrace, rustic, earthy. Perfect for the palette we're going for.

The hole for the pool they dug around the cavity of the missing tree, a vast stretch accessible from several of the rooms.

Now you will have to learn to swim, his wife said.

She was terrified of water, afraid that the children might fall in and drown. Alain did not want a fence obstructing the aesthetics, her husband had agreed. The au pair would have to keep a better eye on the younger ones, he said, that's what she's paid for.

Christmas they spent in Dubai, stayed in a seven-star hotel on a man-made island that was covered in fake snow for the holidays. Saeed had booked it, a thank-you gift for a particularly good weekend. He took the kids shopping, skiing, to theme parks and aquariums. Everything inside, everything in a mall. He liked the sheen of money, new and excessive; the air was hot with it. The hotel staff, Pakis and Filipinos, served him begrudgingly: a black man who was not cleaning toilets, this was against the laws of class and caste. He was used to it, reveled in it even. He gave the kids rolls of dirhams, got them to peel off notes to tip the bellhops and the pool boys so that their shame would be compounded. He bought Zed a Rolex, and a matching one for himself. His wife spent most of the holiday in the hotel room, reading books, watching Arabic soap operas. Go shopping, he said, this is the best place in the world for shopping.

There is nothing left to buy, she said.

When they returned, the house was still not ready. They hosted the New Year's Eve party anyway, erected a marquee in the garden and hired a band. He wore a tuxedo, popped champagne. Shakes arrived with a girl young enough to be his daughter. She teetered on sky-high heels and kept checking to see if her dress was covering her underwear.

My man, Shakes said to him, you did good.

So did you, he replied, and they both laughed.

The guests ogled the house, marveled at the size, and the sparkling pool and the garden, which was illuminated with lanterns. His wife wore the necklace he'd given her for Christmas, thick roped gold with a black diamond in the center. She looked uncomfortable, in the jewelry and her ill-fitting black dress, even inside the house. He looked around at the people in the marquee and felt satisfied with the crowd. Not his friends, but his people nonetheless. The circles he moved in now.

He thought of Mo, who hadn't been invited.

He won't fit in, he told his wife, who said nothing in reply.

You can take the boy out of the township but you can't take the township out of the boy. This was what they said, men like him, over expensive wine in restaurants with waiting lists, because they felt in a position to judge.

He had invited Athene and Alain, the two of them stood huddled in a corner sipping flutes of champagne and surveying the crowd. Every now and then, they giggled, and he wondered what might amuse them so. The mix of money, new and not so new, the pageantry of the recently empowered, intent on removing themselves as far away as possible from the places they had come from. What did it matter? Let them laugh, let them judge. He was here, it was his country, his land, he had the right to grow fat off the riches it offered up. Stake your claim. Take what's yours. Isn't that what everyone else had done, the Dutch and the Portuguese and the English and the Afrikaners, the colonialists and the settlers and the racists who plundered and stole and served no one's interests but their own? The history of the world, rooted not in humanity but in greed. Why should it be any different for him?

It was April when they finally moved in. He walked in and out of the rooms, each one opulent and spacious and sparkling. Everything was new, freshly unpacked and put in place; without memory or emotion, absent of meaning.

At night, he sat on the terrace overlooking the moonlit pool. The suburbs were eerily still, all life contained behind high walls and security fences. His house echoed its silence back at him, and it dawned on him that it would never feel different.

From London, Athene arranged a shoot with *Architectural Digest*. The family sat for a portrait on the white leather sofa, backgrounded by a painting of *The Last Supper* reimagined with an all-black cast of disciples and a dreadlocked Christ. He smiled into the camera and draped an arm over his wife, stiff as wood in a crisp white linen dress picked out by Athene. When the magazine came out, she sent him a framed print of the cover and three copies of the magazine.

Welcome to your new home! she wrote in the note.

He read the article, studied the photographs. In the end, they hadn't used a single shot of the family, just empty rooms, pristine and perfect. The only sign of life in the house was a blurred half-man exiting the kitchen, presumably himself.

RICH MAN DREAMS

What's wrong with the picture is everything. Saeed's fallen asleep with the tigers. Brutus has a paw over his neck, holding fast. Caesar, eyes glazed over and still mourning his balls, is draped morosely over the sofa like one half of a pair of dirty socks.

Ali sighs, approaches slowly lest he wake any one of the beasts. Saeed especially, since he's the most lethal. A murderer and a madman and a king all at once.

Make Your Desert Dreams Come True! These were the words on the brochure that the Chinaman handed Ali on the streets of Udaipur. On the cover, a picture of a smiling Indian couple, color faded so that they'd look white.

Look! the man had said. This future can be yours!

He had a large black mole on the side of his cheek and a cultivated growth of long dark hair sprouting from it. It jumped when he talked, a ventriloquist's puppet. He visited Ali that night at his home, brought a box of *sangam barfi*.

Stay, his wife begged, but her mother wanted a son-in-law with prospects better than those of a roadside *paneer* seller. The Chinaman wore a gold watch on his wrist and a gold ring on his finger. In the center of the ring a ruby sat perched like a perfectly formed drop of blood.

One year, two years—you make more money over there than you make here in ten, he said.

Ali's mother-in-law's eyes glinted. Go, go, she said, a real man provides for his family, a real man has ambition for more than this.

He signed the paper with his birth name and shook the man's hand.

Good, good, the Chinaman smiled, revealing still more gold secreted away inside his rotting black gums. You will not regret this, he said, which was not his first lie, or his last.

Ali doesn't know whether he should get Saeed out first or the tigers. If he leaves the animals sleeping, they'll be restless when they awake. Hungry too. He ought to encourage Saeed's mauling or death by these ridiculous house pets, but he's too afraid of the consequences. He's Saeed's right-hand man. It is his responsibility to keep him safe. Ali pauses a minute and then opts to wake Saeed. He gently taps a finger into his chest. Master Saeed, Master Saeed, he whispers.

Saeed he can smell is fully loaded: drink, cigarettes, whatever drugs he partied with last night all cloying at his pores trying to get out. He reminds Ali of his grandfather, whom he was sent out to recover from the opium dens every Monday morning of his boyhood. His grandfather would be too weak to push him away and too calmed by the drugs coursing through his blood to resist. Ali would drape him over his young shoulders and stumble home to his mother, who'd cluck her tongue and shake her head.

You are a good boy, Sanjai, his grandfather would mumble as he helped him to the mattress on the ground.

It is Ali, Grandfather, he'd say, but the old man would already be asleep.

Ali misses home, misses it like the ache of a severed limb, dull and deep and disorienting to the rest of the body. His parents are long dead, his sisters all married off. It's only himself and his wife, and their child Amita. It is a girl, his mother-in-law had said when the child was brought to him, newly delivered from his wife's belly. Her face was long with disappointment but Ali looked at the baby in his arms and thought she was the most beautiful thing he had ever seen, tiny and sand-colored and all that he had in the world.

She wound a tiny hand around his forefinger and locked herself firmly to him. Amita.

Amita-Baba.

The last night at home before he left, his wife cooked a celebratory meal, all his favorite foods, sweets she'd spent days preparing from scratch in the tiny room in which they ate, slept, and cooked. They invited around their family and friends, in part so that Ali could say his good-byes, in part so that they could make it known to all that the family was soon to become prosperous. His mother-in-law made a toast.

In Dubai, Ali will make his fortune. In Udaipur, we will spend it!

Everyone laughed and Ali thought things might be okay after all, that the sick feeling in his gut might just be nerves at everything unknown that lay ahead.

I don't want you to go, Amita said.

But I am going for you, Ali replied. To make you a better life.

Amita was only six but she looked then like a widow, bereft and broken.

It won't be a better life without you, she said sadly, clinging tightly onto his hand in hers. I will be back soon, Amita, Ali had said. This I promise you.

Ali thinks of his daughter all day and all night, imagines what she might be doing, what his wife might be cooking for their lunch, how his mother-in-law might be scolding her for something she did or didn't do.

Do not forget your reading, he had told Amita before he left. Find as many books as you can. Be good for your mother. Stay out of Naniji's way. No playing before homework.

He wonders if she can still recall his words, or even his voice. She is ten now, almost a woman. She might hardly recognize him.

Natesh had been on the same flight as Ali. He'd had a bright smile and too many dreams to remember.

Know what I'm saving up for? he'd asked Ali. I'm going to open a French bakery! Croissants, tarts with little strawberries, scones and high tea.

Scones aren't French, Ali said, they're English.

Aha, Natesh cried. Your knowledge and my charisma! We could be a dream team.

Ali learned to like Natesh, it was hard not to. They spoke of home and the food their mothers used to cook for them. *Biryani nawabi, amrit phal* with its sweet smell of rose, *lahsooni gosht* so strong it brought tears to the eyes. Ali showed Natesh the photograph he kept of Amita and his wife.

They are beautiful girls, he said.

Natesh took a photo from his own wallet. Look, he said, this is my future wife.

She is promised to you? Ali asked.

Not yet, my friend, Natesh said, but I go back with enough money, and I am confident her father will stop saying no to me.

Natesh came from a long line of disappointing children, with two brothers dead and a sister in disgrace.

An Indian mother, he said, prefers a dead child to an unsuccessful one, nah? At least if they are dead, there is no shame to carry.

His sister, Suhani, had gone to America on a scholarship, married a doctor, become a successful trader. And then she had lost it all.

A blackjack addiction, Natesh told Ali. Can you imagine? They locked her up, her husband paid her bail and bought her a one-way ticket back to India. Thank you and good-bye and good riddance. She came home, my mother locked herself away and cried for a month. Now I am all that is left, Ali, he said, and I must do enough to make up for all of us.

The months passed slowly in Dubai, each one the same as before, only a little more or less excruciatingly hot. New men arrived all the time, each one smiling, each one thinking of the money he would send home or the life he would afford at the end of his stint in the desert. The Chinaman was good at recruiting, not so good afterward. The smiles disappeared fast.

See here, he would show each man an invoice the day after he arrived. Look, this is the cost of your flight, your train, your work permits. This is the agent's fee, for finding you this job. You can pay now or you pay each month, with interest. I take your passport for insurance, I give it back when you owe no money.

The men, exhausted from the journey, bewildered by the oppressive heat and the stink of other men's sweat, had no idea of sums and currencies. They looked at each other and nodded slowly and set off to work.

The average shift was eighteen hours, day in, day out, no breaks, no water. They were contracted to build a hotel, the biggest they'd ever seen. Each week a new floor went up, creeping higher and higher into the clouds while down below the world existed in miniature. From the scaffolding they could peer into apartments, marble and glass blinding them as it caught the sun. Men were already airlifting palm trees in to lay around the perimeter, fully grown trees plucked from the desert to be drilled into holes in the concrete. Six pools, ten restaurants; the closets in the suites were bigger than most of the men's houses back home. The water for the construction was pumped out of enormous pipes, brown and stinking. Still, sometimes when the men could bear the heat no more they stuck their heads under. They collapsed or passed out, there'd be no pay.

The foremen on site were never happy, always yelling, always pushing the men to work harder, faster. They had deadlines, the hotel was already open for bookings. They were usually Australian or South African men, burly and broad with no necks, sweat staining the underarms of their shirts. They looked at plans and shouted into their phones. Their watches were expensive, their cars too. Most of the day they spent in the air-conditioned site office.

The men were shuttled to and from the site in a van that deposited them at the end of the day back to Sonapur. It was a labor camp, guards, barracks. The men slept cheek by jowl on wooden cots lined up against either side of a brick wall. There were fifty men to a bathroom, a toilet and a shower that had only cold water and almost never any soap. Everywhere the reek of rotting waste in the sun, the stench of labor, backbreaking and inhuman. The men were not ashamed to cry out loud at night. They did not console each other, because what was there to say.

Each month that passed the bulk of the wages went into an account.

For your protection, the Chinaman said. So it will grow into more money for you.

The men were given a pittance to live on, barely enough for a meal on the street. They ate rice and vegetables cooked over an open fire by a family of six Filipino sisters who lived in the camp. The younger sisters would consent to a fuck in exchange for lipstick or perfume from the local market. They smiled and twirled their hair, grease from the frying clinging to their skin like they'd been dipped in it.

Ali, back aching, bones creaking, would look every night at the image of his wife and Amita before the lights went out. He couldn't write to them because his wife wasn't able to read. In any case, he couldn't afford the postage. Natesh grew quieter by the day, the smile faded from his lips. He no longer spoke of pastry or the women he wanted to marry.

Cheer up, Ali said. We will get home someday.

Natesh shook his head. No, Ali, there is no way out. We are slaves here till the day we die.

Men hanged themselves in the barracks or jumped from the floors they were building. Sometimes Ali could tell who would be next. The way a man stooped, broken to the core, the way his eyes would look through you to the other side. The Chinaman would be sent to collect the bodies. He'd shake his head and curse under his breath, irate at the loss of a good pair of hands. The body he'd wrap in garbage bags, load into his truck to dump who knows where. The other men shuddered at the sight. No ministrations for the flesh, no *pinda* to appease the spirit of the dead. It stopped some of them, others not. At night, they'd say prayers for the lost men and ask their gods for the strength to endure another day.

This place is built on dead Indians and Pakis, Natesh said. We fill the ground like bricks. Ali, in his darkest moments, pictured himself climbing to the top bunk in the dead of night, fashioning a noose from a piece of cloth, tying it to the beam. He imagined the feeling of sweet release, the moment it all went dark and still; the end of everything that was too much to bear. Then he would see Amita's face, written on it the promise he'd made her. No, he could not do it.

Saeed is looking at him now, trying hard to focus his doped-up eyes. Brutus yawns at his ear but stays asleep; the breath on him carnivorous and stale.

Come, Master Saeed, Ali urges. You must come away from the tigers now.

Saeed's eyes suddenly are wide and excited as he recognizes Ali.

But they are so cuddly, Ali! Like the little fluffy toys kids keep on their pillow. And see, mine are real!

He laughs loudly, no fear, no sense, all of it snorted out through his nose or never there to begin with. Ali takes him by the arm, pulls him up. His leg accidentally kicks into Caesar's belly and the animal wakes with a start. He leaps up onto his haunches, growls loudly, licks his teeth. Ali can see his heart beating against his fur, ready for action.

Saeed, moronic, maniacal, laughs. Ali, you have woken the king! Now he will be a grouch all day.

Ali takes in a breath, holds out a hand. Everybody nice and calm, he instructs. Master, I implore you to please stay very still now.

His voice is a lullaby, Caesar eyes the men, then decides to sit back down.

Ali keeps his hand out, his voice calm. Yes, that is a good boy, sit down, Caesar, sit down like a good boy.

When the animal is no longer agitated, he motions with his hand for Saeed to leave. Come, Master, it would be best for you to leave the room now.

Saeed giggles, allows himself to be ushered out.

In his bedroom, Ali lays him carefully atop the bed. The headboard is made of real gold.

Where are my whores, Ali? Saeed asks. I hope you did not chase them away with your sad eyes. He laughs again, he likes to tease.

No, Master Saeed, Ali replies. The women are only in the room next door.

It's true that there are women, but also girls as young as twelve and boys who look like girls. Saeed likes a mix of pleasures. He yawns and rolls onto his side. Actually, he says, you can send them home now. I am finished with them. And they always smell in the morning, like fish left in the sun.

He closes his eyes and Ali slips out of the room.

He's been Saeed's valet for just over a year now. Saeed calls him his valet, because he likes the word and he likes to fashion himself as an English gentleman. Really, Ali is a slave. But Saeed likes him, or at least he likes to toy with him and make him do the repulsive things he knows will appall him. Anything he asks, Ali replies, of course, Master Saeed. Saeed sometimes orders Ali to accompany him on what he calls his shopping trips. He visits schools in the neighborhood just as classes are coming out. Her, maybe her, not her friend—she has a Jew's nose, he will say. He picks and chooses girls, then Ali is sent to find out their names. Their mothers are sent gift baskets as a token of Saeed's appreciation for their daughters' beauty. The girls who end up pregnant are taken care of by Saeed's personal physician, the ones who commit suicide have handsome compensation sent to their families. Ali arranges it all.

Saeed's father inherited oil and land enough to make him rich beyond measure, but his son reminds him that he is poor where it counts. There are no grandchildren; no pride in an heir who is a drunk and a playboy and a shameful Muslim. Seven cars, one for every day of the week, a palace lined wall to wall with gold, servants to tend to his every need, girls to fuck, boys to party with, and still Saeed is unsatisfied with life. Bored, morose. The only things that make him happy are the cats, who roam free in the grounds since Saeed refuses to chain them up.

They are my favorite pussies in the world, Ali, he says. How could I treat them like prisoners?

Saeed thinks that the reason the cats don't attack him is out of love. The real reason is that Ali keeps them sedated with tranquilizers. Caesar he had neutered last week while Saeed was in London attending the sales. The vet said it would make the tiger listless, less inclined to hunt. So far he's just been a grouch. The rest of the staff doesn't mind keeping the secret, they don't want to be devoured by a tiger any more than Ali does. Most of them are like him anyway, far from home, worked around the clock to keep Saeed happy. There's a young Bengali who reminds him a little of Natesh. When he speaks to him, Ali has to look away.

It was just before Ramadan when Natesh started smiling for the first time in years.

Ali, he said, I know how we can get out of here.

Ali was used to talk of escape and freedom but not from Natesh, not in a long time. He looked over at his friend.

Tell me, he said, what is your plan?

Plan is flawless, my friend. Guaranteed to work.

Natesh was so excited he couldn't sit.

Go on, Ali said. What is this idea you've cooked up for us?

Listen, Natesh said. Muneeb told me how it works. His cousin Murad did it and now he's sitting pretty back at home in Khammam with his wife by his side and two million rupees in his pocket. No lies, Ali, no fairy tale. Just a little bit of genius.

Ali listened. Natesh told him the story of how Murad had gotten himself hit by the car of a drunken Arab outside a nightclub.

So you see, he said, no Emirati wants his license taken away—who's gonna drive the Lamborghini? So he hits some poor Paki and he wants to make it go away nice and quick before the police come. What does he do? Dips into the glove box for his pocket money and pays him to disappear. No charges, no fines. He can drive off to the next club, find some girls to bang till dawn. Meanwhile Paki takes his gammy leg and his money, pays off his boss, gets his passport back, and goes home. Home, Ali! Natesh said, eyes shining, full of promise, full of hope.

What do you think, he said. Sounds good, nah? Sounds like a plan.

Ali wanted to share the excitement, but felt only dread.

Natesh, Natesh, he shook his head. It's too risky. What if you get badly hurt, not just a scratch for show. What if the person who hits you doesn't have enough money to get you home. It is a gamble, he said, and much worse than Suhani's blackjack. You forget that this is Dubai, rules here do not work in our favor, my friend. It is too dangerous. There is too much to go wrong.

But Natesh was not to be dissuaded. Ali, he said, look at me. Listen to me. If I don't do this, I will check out the other way. And you, he went on, you will be the one to cut my body down from that beam.

It needed to happen soon, before Ramadan started. They chose a Friday, watched the van load the men up after their shift and drive them away. From the building site, Ali and Natesh walked. Around them the cranes towered overhead. Another hotel, so tall they said you'd see it from space. Apartment blocks like ghost towns, unlived in and unloved. Look at this place, Natesh said, everything shining, everything new. But nothing is real. Nothing but us, and the blood we spill building them their fucking Disneyland of the desert.

Natesh had some money saved up from the pitiful weekly allowance.

Come, he said. Tonight we will pretend that we are rich men. They walked into an American restaurant, chose a table at the window. They ordered cheeseburgers, fries, two large sodas. The waiter, Sri Lankan or Keralan by the looks of him, eyed the men suspiciously, doubtful they could afford to pay for the meal. He pointed to the menu with his finger hovering over the price.

This one, sir? It is eighteen dirhams.

Yes, Natesh said. This is the one.

The sodas came and Natesh held up his glass. We will be home soon, Ali, he said, home where we belong.

Ali's stomach turned. Inshallah, he said, and they both laughed.

Inshallah, Natesh echoed, his hands together in mock prayer.

Ali was going to be the witness. His job was to create enough fuss around the accident so that negotiations could take place before the police arrived on the scene. In return, Natesh promised him all the money he needed to pay off his debt and buy a return flight to Udaipur. They'd shaken hands on it.

We'll make it, Ali, Natesh said, and Ali nodded.

They ate their food and watched the night come to life. Cars pulled up, dispensed robed and turbaned men, women with heavily painted faces and sky-high heels. The hotel bars and clubs would be filling up. Ali and Natesh waited, ordered more sodas to appease the waiter, who frowned every time he passed by the table knowing he'd get no tip for his troubles. Around eleven, they paid and left, took up a position on a busy corner where they could watch the action. A man screeched to a halt in a yellow Porsche, stumbled out with two women who spoke with heavy Australian accents.

Look, Natesh said. He's a good one.

They waited, crouched like hunters in the dark.

What if this doesn't work, Natesh, Ali asked.

Natesh shrugged and smiled. Ali, he said, it must work. There is nothing else to try.

Everything that happened next, Ali can recall in the minutest detail: the sound of the tires hitting flesh, the smell of blood, black and metallic, the taste of bile in his mouth as he looked at the mangled body of his friend. The man driving the yellow Porsche was raging.

Fucking brand-new wheels, he shouted at Ali, brand-new, custom-made. You know how long you wait for that?

Ali, holding Natesh, didn't know where to put his hands, where to press to stop the blood pumping out of the body of his friend. Natesh was soaked through.

Please, please, Ali cried, look at what you have done. He needs an ambulance, he needs help. Please sir, please.

He didn't care about the plan, didn't care about the money or even getting home. People who came out of the bars gathered around, looking to see what the commotion was. Fuck, he's in bad shape, man, someone said. Still, no one moved to help.

The driver, coked up, paced back and forth, pulling at his hair.

Fuck, fucking Christ.

He looked around, then said to Ali, okay, come, bring him.

Ali nodded, lifted Natesh, tried not to hurt him as he hoisted him and draped him over his shoulders. The man opened the passenger door for him to climb in.

You're going to help him? Ali asked.

Yes, the man said, just get in.

Ali sat, Natesh on top of him, blood seeping slowly out of one man and into the next. The man drove fast, all over the road. Drunk or high or both.

We are going to the hospital? Ali asked.

The man was silent. They drove, it seemed like an hour. Eventually he pulled off the road and stopped the car.

We are here, he said. Bring him.

Ali eased Natesh off him gently and squeezed out from under him. From outside the car, he bent, gripped him under his arms, and lifted. Natesh against him felt cool to the touch, his breath no more than a whisper against Ali's cheek.

You'll be okay, Natesh, he whispered. Home is waiting. Home is waiting. Just hang on, my friend, please hang on.

He looked up, looked around. Expected to see a hospital and saw instead that they were in the middle of nowhere.

Sir, he said, please sir, where is the hospital? Where is the help for this man you have injured?

The man, pacing again, wild-eyed and fevered, shook his head.

No, he said, no hospital I'm afraid. Too risky. Too many questions. Fuck, he said. What a fucking night.

He leaned into the car, pulled something from the glove box, walked over to where Ali sat crouched over Natesh, trying in vain to keep him conscious.

Okay, he said. It's decision time.

In his hand, a gun, pointed squarely at Ali's head.

You have two options, he said. You can roll hamburger patty over here down this embankment and come with me, or I can leave you both here. A bullet for you, a bullet for him. Nice and simple.

Ali, stunned, confused, tried to figure out what was happening. But he is hurt, he said. He needs a doctor. Please, sir. Please. This is a good man. This is my friend. This is not a man who should die.

He was pleading for Natesh's life but to the wrong man, because this man had no concern for human life, not even a trace.

The man waved the gun, impatient. Yes, yes, he said. I am sure he is a saint. But my father always told me that good boys clean up their mess. And I think you will agree that this is a very big mess.

He laughed a maniacal laugh, feral and piercing like a knife in the night. Around Ali, a void of darkness echoed it back over sand and sky, a nightmare without end.

Caesar and Brutus are restless now. Ali can hear them pacing the floor in the room next door; hungry, always hungry. He needs to get them fed and drugged for the day. But first he needs to send the others home.

He opens the door to what Saeed calls his parlor, peers inside. Bottles, syringes, underwear on the floor, bodies draped over furniture in the places where they passed out. He flies them in sometimes, models and actresses, mostly Russians who will do anything for money. Occasionally, the South African will arrive with lithe black women in sparkly dresses. If he likes them he'll send them home with a little box from Tiffany's, keeps a stash of them like candy in his bedroom drawer. One girl, naked, barely a teenager, rocks back and forth on the floor; coming down or doing whatever it is they do the day after.

Ali lifts her; come, he says, the driver will take you back to your hotel.

He finds a blanket, drapes it over her shoulders, tries not to notice the bruises on her body, the stain of blood marking her thigh like a snail's sticky trail. The others he wakes slowly, polite as always. He calls Jamal to bring up a pot of coffee, gets them moving a little quicker. One by one, they leave, Saeed's regular hangers-on back to their own compounds, the party girls mostly straight to the airport to catch the next flight out.

In the kitchen, Ali gets them to prepare the tigers' breakfast. Raw fillet steak they eat while the staff exists on rice and beans. Jamal brings up the bowls, greets Ali with a smile like he always does. Ali slips the tranquilizers into the meat, presses them into the bloody flesh. He listens outside the door, then opens up. Caesar and Brutus eye him with suspicion, bare their teeth, lick their lips. They know it's Ali keeping them fed, keeping them drugged.

Masters, Ali says, your breakfast is served.

He slides the two bowls over and the tigers leap toward them, growling, ravenous. They devour the meat in seconds, blood dripping from their teeth, red marking their fur. They look at Ali, wanting more, always wanting more. The tranquilizers kick in quick, the tigers already lethargic and slow as they skulk back to the couch.

Seven months ago, Saeed fed a man to them, alive and screaming. The tigers tore him in two, arms one way, legs another, muscles and ligaments snapping like Christmas crackers. The man screamed for his life, then for mercy, the staff looking on in horror. Saeed stood and watched, stone cold like marble, bored after a few minutes. He took out his phone while the tigers finished the job. It took Jamal a week to wipe the bloodstains from the floors and the walls, each day he'd spot something he'd missed, particles of flesh and plasma. Now the tigers have a taste for human flesh. They want blood, guts, bones to crunch. The fillet they eat, but not with relish. Their time will come. They watch, they wait. Ali watches them too. The way they move, every fiber of their being regal and commanding, afraid of nothing, answerable to no one. Kings. And still, they are slaves like him. Trapped, powerless. A plaything for a wayward prince. But look in their eyes and you can't miss it. It's written, clear as day, burning bright, fueling every miserable day of this miserable life. Yes, one day soon, any day now, they will make their move.

And so will he. In another two hundred and thirty-eight days to be exact. He will do it, he knows he will. Because his plan demands nothing more of him than time, and Ali is used to waiting. Saeed wears a brand-new pair of Calvin Klein boxer shorts every day. The previous day's pair he tosses into the trash can in the bathroom, where Ali fishes them out, hides them in his pocket, and takes them back to his room at the end of each day to wash and dry. He folds them carefully, returns them to the original packaging, which he keeps in a stash in the little cupboard beside his bed. Then he gives them to Jamal's cousin Kaleem, who comes by once a week to deliver to Saeed a crate of whiskey bought off a New Zealander with an expat alcohol license. Kaleem sells the boxers at the souk, two for the price of one, half for Ali, half for him. The money he hides in a newspaper and hands back to Ali, who secrets it away in a tight roll in his pillow. Every week, there is a little more money. Soon, there'll be just enough. He'll buy a ticket, he'll pay the man who is making him a new passport. He'll wait for Saeed to dismiss him for the evening, or pass out cold, whichever comes first. Then he will check on the tigers one last time, and leave. He will be a free man, a new man. This place, this prison, will belong only to the past.

From the other room, he can hear Saeed calling. He closes the door behind the tigers and goes to him.

Ali, Ali, Saeed whines. My head hurts.

Ali fetches a cloth from the bathroom and wipes Saeed's brow. He gives him two aspirin and a glass of water, holds the glass to his lips as he sips.

Ali, Saeed says, my loyal valet. You are the only man for the job.

Yes sir, Ali says, it is an honor.

He puts a pillow behind Saeed and pulls the covers over him.

It must have been fate that brought us together, no? Saeed says.

He always grows sentimental with a hangover.

Yes, Master Saeed, Ali says, it was surely fate.

Saeed is looking up at him now in the way a child looks at his father.

Do you think I am a bad man, Ali? he asks.

Ali's mind can't help itself. He plays back the scene, same one over and over again. Natesh, dropping slowly over the embankment, rolling, rolling, moaning or weeping or maybe just silent, it was impossible to hear over Ali's own screams, guttural and animal-like.

He'll be dead either way, Saeed had said, just look at him.

Afterward, he patted Ali on the back and smiled. Good, good. You are good at cleaning up my mess. I think we will be a fine team.

Ali, Ali? Saeed's voice again, pleading, pathetic. Am I a bad man?

Ali looks at Saeed, crumpled on the bed, eyes bloodshot from drugs and sleeplessness, veins bruised from too many needles, pores reeking of a thousand sins. Ali puts on a smile, big and wide.

Oh Master Saeed, he says. You are the best kind of man there is.

Saeed smiles slowly, closes his eyes, readies himself for oblivion. And what kind of man is that, Ali? he asks.

Ali draws the curtains, shuts out the light.

Rich, he says. You are rich.

IT'S NOT REALLY A CULT

She saw him approaching and realized it was too late to make an escape. Tom, Tom the Toff, in his white linen slacks and slicked back too-blond hair. He came up beside her, touched her lightly on the arm. The tiny hairs stood on end, she realized he repulsed her.

Didn't mean to startle you, he cooed.

You didn't, she said.

It's wonderful, isn't it? This setting, Guru Sri. Enlightening, really, in the true sense of the word.

He seemed oblivious to her disinterest, kept talking at her while she held her book and tried to look as though she were midsentence.

Ah, Deepak Chopra, he said, reading the cover. Good base to work from, nice pedestrianized kind of spirituality. Accessible, he added. He lay back in the chair beside her, rested his hands behind his head, and looked out toward the sea.

So you're here why? he asked. Divorce, heartbreak, death? I can't tell with you. Usually I can tell.

I'm here for the quiet actually, she said coldly, removing her sunglasses for emphasis.

Fuck me, he said. You're beautiful. I saw earlier, but up close.

Are you hitting on me? she said. You're actually hitting on me.

Maybe, he said, yeah.

Jesus, seriously? Athene said, isn't that, I don't know, kind of fucking counterintuitive.

To what, Tom said.

To this! This place and the teachings, and well, fuck, everything.

Tom looked at her, slight smirk on his face. You don't seem to be embracing Guru Sri's teachings, he said. Universal love. The flow of energies. Life forces.

He stood up and shrugged. Too bad, he said, I feel that you could use a bit of a shift, maybe clear some of those blockages that are holding you back.

He walked away, left her raging. Raging that she was raging. He was right. She was not embracing the teachings she had paid a lot of money to be entitled to embrace.

She didn't know what it was, why she couldn't relax. Release. Let go, let God. All that stuff she was trying to absorb, Deepak Chopra at her side, Guru Sri in front, multitude of believers everywhere else, chanting and oming and awash with the Attitude of Gratitude. She'd met a French architect on a job in Cape Town. He raved about the retreat. Guru Sri, he said, she will change your life. This is what she wanted, a changed life, one different and better than her own. She paid the deposit, booked the flight to Goa, handed her keys to her neighbor and assured her that she would not die in a flood or a tsunami (though she herself was not convinced), packed a backpack for the very first time in her life, and left. And for what. It wasn't Zen she was feeling, it was irritation. Infuriation. The food was awful, the rooms a far cry from what she had seen online. Guru Sri she found unsettling, the fellow attendees pretentious. And then there was fucking Tom. She sighed deeply, knowing she'd need to apologize. Make amends in the spirit of loving-kindness. Make space for the magic to happen. Christ, she was ill-suited to all this. She scanned the garden for him, sure he'd be chatting up someone else.

He was alone, sitting cross-legged in meditation mode. She walked over, the grass sharp underfoot. Standing in front of him she clenched and unclenched her jaw.

Sorry, she said. Not really feeling in the zone today.

Baby steps, he said. You'll get there.

He patted the lawn next to him, indicating that she should sit.

The air was hot and sticky, her yoga pants clung to her underwear, soupy and foul. The smells that came from her here were something else. The underwear she'd worn on the flight over she ended up throwing into the trash.

Come, Tom said again, sit.

She sat, tried not to feel so disdained by it all.

Amelia? he said.

Athene.

Of course, he said, sorry. This your first?

She nodded.

It takes time, he said. You can't really rush it. Everything happens in its own time, just as it should. The perfection of the universe's timing.

Jesus, she said. You're like a pocket edition.

Well, I've done a few of these, he said. More than a few.

So you're a full-fledged member of the cult, she said.

He shrugged. You know what they say, he said. The only difference between a religion and a cult? About a hundred years.

The horn sounded for lunch and they got up to go to the ballroom. The retreat was run from an original manor house dating back to 1682, Portuguese tiles lining the walls, a grand staircase, an avenue of ashokas either side of the drive. It was unrestored, crumbling. A vestige of a bygone era of aristocrats and governor's balls. Now Goa was full of stoners and hippies, sun worshippers and seekers of Hindu wisdom neatly wrapped for the masses. The beaches were lined with bars and restaurants that catered to generic tourist tastes. Hamburgers and banana splits and tragically watered-down Indian food. You were hard-pressed to find an authentic. Goan curry. Any charm the place once had was gone. Cheap and tacky, that's all it was now.

Lunch at the retreat was the same every day. Aubergine curry, rice, sliced tomatoes, pineapple for dessert. Everyone sat together at the long table, said a prayer of thanks, and ate mostly in silence. Athene hated the sound of other people's chewing. Tom beside her ate with his hands, slurped the food in noisy mouthfuls that grated at her nervous system in profound ways. Misophonia, it was called, a loathing so strong it constituted a neuropsychiatric disorder.

Tom wiped his mouth with his sleeve. So good, right? he said.

She chewed, nodded.

You know, the time will come, he said, the time is not far off when you won't even be able to buy this stuff anymore.

What? she said.

Tomatoes, pineapple.

It's the bees, he went on. Dying in droves. Ten million beehives every year. Poof! Wiped out. No bees, he said, no pollination. No pollination, no crops. He dished a second helping of curry and continued with the chewing.

You're pretty morbid for someone so full of universal love, Athene said.

He shook his head. No, he said. Morbid is not the word. Realistic is what I am. And at the same time—who cares? Endings and beginnings, collapse and rebirth, love and hate. Energy. Love. It's all the same, baby, flowing along, no matter what we say or do or pray for. The wonders of the universe. Magic and profane. Life, not what we make of it, but what it makes of us. Am I right?

She wondered if he was high, looked at his eyes for telltale signs but found none. She decided she'd fuck him, not yet sure of the reason why.

In the afternoon there was a silent meditation on the lawn. She sat next to Tom on one side and Kitty on the other. She hated Kitty, for being called Kitty, for having the legs to pull off nude leggings. She wondered if Tom had noticed too. Her friend Fern told her the retreat would be a waste of time. The only women you'll meet will be tragic and wounded, the only men you'll meet are the ones looking to take advantage of them. Athene thought she was jealous. She was still trying to make a go of her handmade jewelry business; her disposable income was unchanged since their student days. In fact, she lived with students, flat sharing in a shit hole in Shoreditch like she was a girl of twenty instead of a woman on the wrong side of thirty. On nights Athene wanted to go out, she usually ended up paying for them both. London prices never came cheap. They'd start with a nice dinner, ceviche or dim sum, something light, and then head to one of the hotel bars where the cocktails were pink and came with nuts. They'd sit, titter, wait to get picked up. One night they ended up in a shisha lounge on Edgeware Road, drinking mint tea and sharing a plate of baklava with two Emirati business-men. They had been in negotiations to go back to their hotel rooms when a custom yellow Porsche pulled up. The men smiled, said something to each other in Arabic.

Saeed is here, the one man said. You like his car? He flies it from Dubai so he can drive it when he is visiting London!

The man in the Porsche opened the door and yelled. The oth-er men shrugged, turned to Athene and Fern, and told them they would need to leave. Fern was devastated, already she had notions of being a kept woman, mistress to an oil sheik.

In general London frustrated Athene, feeling always too gritty or too polished for her liking. Still, she wasn't around much anyway. Her apartment on Talbot Road—tasteful, uncluttered—looked like one of those show flats they used to sell new apartments off-plan. She felt the echo of the empty walls and her unlived-in anthracite Hay sofa. Sometimes she struggled to recall where the mugs were kept. She collected voyager miles she never used. She bought expensive lightweight luggage, made of carbon or some-thing similarly revolutionary. She kept champagne in her fridge, vodka in the freezer, for just in case. The bottles remained un-opened.

When she was in London, she preferred to work from the Electric, sat at one of the tables with her laptop and her books of notes, drank fresh pomegranate juice, and ordered the smashed avocado on toast if she was allowing herself carbs. She liked to people-watch, the models, the pseudocreatives with their hard drives filled with abandoned screenplays, the odd minor celebrity, men in orange loafers, hardened producers barking orders down a phone. She eavesdropped on conversations, whispered confessions of affairs with married men, discussions on divorce settlements and how to get one's children into the best private schools. Occasionally, she'd get hit on, though seldom by anyone she had any interest in knowing. Most Englishmen bored her to tears, either too wellborn or too painfully common.

My work keeps me terribly busy, she usually said, a few dates down the line; badly chosen films and a dinner or two split down the middle. They understood, they stopped calling. Sometimes she wished that they wouldn't.

Your problem is you can't make up your mind about what you want, Fern said, her attempt at wisdom.

There was a chance that she was right. On paper, she had pretty much everything it was that she wanted. But still, the feeling she associated most with her life was emptiness.

She studied Guru Sri in front of her on the lawn, tried to figure out what it was she disliked about her. She longed for a steak, for sushi, and that Bircher muesli from Whole Foods. She still had a bag of biltong with her from South Africa. She ate from it at night, under cover of darkness, a fugitive carnivore.

Beautiful beings, before we close this afternoon's self-heal meditation, let us go deep, let us find the places the trauma lurks . . . feel it. Acknowledge it.

Hello trauma.

Hello trauma, everyone echoed.

Everything in your body, Guru Sri said, everything is a guest. This means you can tell it when to stay and when to go.

Good-bye trauma! everyone shouted.

Athene pictured the other unwanted guests that had taken up residence in her body of late: the gray pubic hairs, five of them and counting, the puckered skin of her chest, the age spot on her hand. Fern had started Botox, used up her meager savings to freeze her eggs. Warding off the apocalypse, she called it. Athene had modeled once, stood in front of a row of women who pinched her thighs to check for cellulite. Had she been beautiful then? It was hard to know.

Athene realized what she found unsettling about Guru Sri. It was the accent. American. She closed her eyes and waited for the session to finish. Her knees were cramping. Guru Sri ended with a chant, walked between them and sprayed each head with a squirt of something that smelled of oranges and frankincense.

This is Hindu truth serum, she said, breathe it in, let it open you like a flower.

Later that night, Tom cupping her breast with his hand, Athene felt the weight of her failure.

This isn't what I'm supposed to be discovering here, she said.

Of course it is, Tom assured her. Every experience you experience is what you're meant to experience.

No, Christ, she said. Come on. For a minute. I'm already in the sack. Be real with me.

I am being real, he said.

He was running his fingers through her pubic hair. A full bush, he'd commented earlier when she'd undressed, you don't see many of those in your demographic anymore.

He tugged at her hair now. Real, he said, real as real.

Get out of my fucking bed, she replied.

No, no, wait, okay. Okay.

They could hear the sounds of a beach party outside, full moon or quarter moon. Whatever excuse they could find. Athene thought about her youth, not enough of it misspent on tropical beaches. Not enough of it misspent at all. In the morning, the sand would be littered with empty beer bottles and paper lanterns, burned out and discarded.

Right now, I'd love a cigarette, Tom said.

He was English like her, a Londoner, or maybe a northerner with an accent hidden in the wings. During a project in the States, Athene had learned that the Americans were as class obsessed as the British. Her client was an Upper East Side trophy wife, tan and lean and coiffed to within an inch of her life. Her husband paid her a thousand dollars for every pound she lost after giving birth to their son. She was using the money to redecorate the house. Athene observed her in the stores, choosing fabrics and vases, asking if the console tables were mahogany or cherry. She fitted the part to perfection. In the car on the way back to the house, she'd taken a call.

I'm sorry, she said, I need to take this.

Suddenly she was someone else. All *tawk* and *cawr* and *cawfee*. When she hung up, she turned to Athene.

My sister, she said, accent like before. We grew up in Long Island. I talk to her like I talk to everyone else, she'll come over here and punch my lights out.

Athene understood. Hours of practice, maybe a dialect coach. Movies from the forties. Talking aloud in front of the mirror. Eventually it would stick. The other stuff too, hand gestures and gait. It was like the homes she decorated, transformation only ever a few carefully chosen swathes of fabric away.

Tom was out of bed, examining the doors and windows to see if he could smoke undetected.

Don't, she said. Guru Sri might sacrifice you to the gods.

He sniggered, what on earth would the gods want with the likes of me. No, okay, he said. So you wanted real.

Yes, she said.

He climbed back into bed, resumed position with his hands on her breasts. You might not like it, he said.

Tell me anyway.

Uh, he said. Truth is, yes. I come to these things to meet women.

Athene laughed, found it pitiful and quaint at the same time. But why, she said, you're not a hunchback. You can form basic sentences.

M'lady charms me so, he said. He kissed her neck.

Seriously, she said. Why not stay home, go to a bar, take up salsa? Get on bloody Tinder, she said. OkCupid. Match.com. She couldn't think of any more she'd tried. Disasters all.

I suppose, he said. But, these places are something special. Something different. The women here . . .

They're vulnerable! she said, feeling so now. And you're deceiving them. It's not fair, she said.

Athene, he said. He rolled her onto her back so she would look at him. In the moonlight, his hair was white, a halo around his head.

We are all vulnerable, he said. And we are all deceiving each other all the time.

The next day, she reported him after breakfast.

You are the head prefect, Guru Sri smiled. You want what exactly to happen? she asked.

Athene was affronted. He's here for the wrong reasons, she said.

And what are the right reasons? Guru Sri asked, voice like caramel.

Athene threw up her hands. I don't know, she said. For enlightenment, to learn, to take a break from life.

Tom, out of the corner of her eye, she noticed coming toward them. Sri gestured with her hand for him to join them.

You have upset Athene, Sri said. She feels you are not being honest.

Not true, he said. I am being honest. I told her I come to these places to meet women.

Oh please, Athene said, this is now so juvenile.

She felt embarrassed, chastised like a child.

Sri smiled at her. And you are here for the honest reason of . . . ?

Athene looked around, Kitty doing downward dogs just for shits and giggles, the others meditating or sipping ginger tea and talking in soft voices about karma and the disembodied spirit.

Jesus, she said, I don't know. To get away I suppose.

From your life? Guru Sri asked, voice still full of calm.

Yes, she said.

But then we have a breakthrough here! Sri cried. Because what life is it that you need to escape? The life that is not your true path, that's what.

Athene sighed, no, she said, my life is fine, I just wanted some—I don't know.

You are happy, in this life? Sri asked.

Happy enough, she said.

Guru Sri looked deeply offended. She got up to walk away.

This answer you give me, she said, makes me believe that you are the one who is being dishonest.

Athene, horrified, turned to Tom. What the fuck? she said.

She has a point, he shrugged.

Still smiling. Not insulted, just amused. His eyes were clear, nothing lurking behind them.

Come, he said, let's use our free time this morning for a beer.

They left the others, Kitty horrified that they weren't staying for the drum circle she'd arranged. The walk to the beach was not far. On the main road, they found a stall selling American junk food. Athene bought a Snickers bar, Tom cigarettes.

What is this doing to our chakras, she said, what evil will this chocolate unleash upon my flesh?

Tom wagged his finger at her. You can mock, he said, but she hit a nerve, didn't she?

Athene took a bite, chewed, thought. Maybe, she said.

They approached the beach via one of the hotels. There was a couple ahead of them, her hand on the back of his shirt, his hand under her backside.

Jesus, Athene said, he's literally cupping her urethra.

It's called affection, Tom said. He reached down to remove his sandals. You're angry, you know, he said. Like, boiling-over angry, just with the lid still on the pot.

Well this place isn't helping, she said.

The waiter at the nearest beach bar waved them over. The bar was nestled between three large palm trees in the sand. Two stoned-looking tourists lay in hammocks below a Pepsi sign, a woman swept the sand off the tables with a palm frond. The place was called Tiki-La's. One thousand kinds of tequila! the menu boasted. Athene wondered if that was possible. The waiter offered them lattes, American pancakes, strawberry daiquiris. Globalization, the gradual saming of the world.

They ordered two Kingfishers, no ice, a plate of fried potatoes.

Bet Sri will feel this, Athene said, register it right in the heart center or wherever it is you're supposed to feel things.

Tom took a drink of the beer, looked out at the sea, which was calm and turquoise and inviting. Athene realized that she had not yet been in the water.

You're missing the whole point, Athene, he said. It isn't about anyone being right or having the answers or solving the problems of your life. It's just, you know, a space. An opening.

An opening? she said. Do you mean my vagina?

She was feeling giddy, the beer, the sun, maybe the telling off from Sri earlier.

Tom laughed. She realized with a certain horror that she liked him. There was a naturalness to him. She envied it.

Is it me or is Sri kind of cunty?

Athene speared a couple of potatoes onto a fork and shoved them into her mouth. The oil they'd been fried in was old and dirty but the grease was welcome nonetheless.

I mean, I am a paying guest, she huffed.

Actually, Tom said, I think the two of you are more alike than you may think.

Jesus, thanks, she said.

Tom finished his beer, ordered another. Guru Sri, he said, she's no guru.

Athene rolled her eyes, well clearly, she said.

No, Tom said, listen. A few years ago, she was this wunderkind trader in the States, a real hotshot. Then she discovered blackjack, developed some kind of serious addiction. She gambled everything away—everything. Lost the savings, the house, the car. Husband. Everything was gone. She had nothing in the world.

So she's a fraud, Athene yelped, a con artist?

Wait, Tom said, you need the whole story. Let me finish.

Athene speared more potatoes onto her fork, shoved it theatrically into her mouth to shut herself up.

So, Tom continued, in India, these kids that leave, these scientists and doctors and lawyers who study abroad and make a life for themselves unlike anything their parents could ever dream possible, the pressure for them is something else. There's no fucking it up. Because it isn't just their life, you understand, it's the life of their parents and their grandparents and their less-bright siblings who never got the chance to get out—it's for all of them. So Sri, when she failed so almightily, when she wrecked her whole world, well, it was like a death. She was dead to her parents, dead to her community. She had basically two options, stay dead and do like most fallen women do—clean toilets, suck cocks—or start again. Start from scratch. New life, new self, new everything. So that's what she did. All of this—this is business. Because she's no fool—she knows dumb-fuck foreigners with money and vacant souls, they'll pay good money to find their spiritual redemption in a far-away place with someone who has the word *guru* in her name. But she also knows something about life, about loss and grief and the transience of happiness—the stuff that the people who come here are crippled with. It's a win-win situation. She's managed to redeem herself, she sends money home to her mother, who no longer tells people her daughter is dead, she has somewhere to live and a website and a place in the world again. And the people who come here—for the most part, anyway—they leave feeling good about their lives, wiser and more grounded and able to cope with whatever it is waiting for them back home.

A kind of placebo effect, Athene said.

Maybe. Or maybe an actual remedy. In that you allow yourself to be someone else when you are away from home, when you have the space for a more honest self, perhaps. A self who is open to change or healing or whatever.

Well, you've clearly drunk the Kool-Aid, Athene said.

Tom shrugged. It's how I feel. It's why I come to these things. That, and the women of course, he said, giving her a wink.

But how do you know all this, about Sri?

We exchanged some truths, he said. Bit of hers, bit of mine. I think we understand each other.

Athene snorted, she understands that you come looking to get laid?

Tom smiled. Everyone's looking for something.

They sat awhile, saying nothing. Athene played with a sachet of sugar, emptied the grains onto the table, and shaped the wrapper into a little bird. She thought of her trip to Zagreb last summer. On a day off from her project, she'd stumbled into a place called the Museum of Broken Relationships, a shrine to lost love filled with donated objects that represented people's greatest heartbreaks. Garden gnomes, guitars, corks. Even condom wrappers. At the time she'd wondered if there would ever be anything of hers worth donating. A love worth remembering; some useless object laden with private meaning and grief.

Learning to fly? Tom asked.

Perhaps, she said.

The sun was warm on her back. She dug her feet into the sand. She felt far away from everything, close to something else. She slipped the bird into her purse.

Come, Tom said. He put several notes on the table and stood up, took her hand, led her to the edge of the water.

We're going in, he said.

He threw his shirt on the sand. She peeled off her dress, clammy against her back, followed him into the warmth of the Indian Ocean. The water made way for her and she lay on her back, arms spread, legs keeping her gently afloat. She closed her eyes, breathed in the sun and the sky and the stillness. The water filled her ears and she heard the strange echo of the sea mixed with her own internal workings, heart and pulse and synapses, as she bobbed in a gentle embrace of water and time.

After what seemed like a long while, she went under, tasted salt, felt the sting of seawater on her lips and in her eyes. She stayed under until all breath was gone and a while after that. The instinct to breathe forced her to the surface, she broke the water with a gasp and the air rushed at her and an arm found its way around her waist.

On the flight home, she paged through the duty-free catalogue from the seat in front of her. There was a game you could buy for $9.99, several dice with different pictures on each one. You took the dice, shook them, scattered them. The random pictures that they landed on were the ones you used to build your story.

STONE BABY

Madame Monique of Riad Bovary in Fez, a once-beautiful French-woman who didn't seem to object to the waning of her youth or beauty, was up every morning at six A.M. It was always the same. She rose, drank the strong coffee prepared for her by Hassan and brought to her door on a silver tray, wrapped a scarf around her neck, and went downstairs. It was her favorite time of day. Too early for the guests to be up or for the rest of the staff to arrive. Only stillness, silence; the soft rattling of Hassan in the kitchen and the song of the swifts in the orange trees outside.

The sight of the riad in the morning light took her breath away. It was magnificent, the crumbling walls, the chipped remains of mosaics—everything meticulously restored and returned to its former glory. It made her feel like Scheherazade, installed in a palace, a living work of art. It had taken years and almost all her money, but she'd refused to stop until the place gleamed. A testament to her love of the city. A testament to love itself, which was more or less the same thing. She had visited the Taj Mahal some months ago on a trip to India. She wanted to see what Shah Jahan had built with his grief, this wonder of the world and the great monument to overwhelming love and despair at his wife Mumtaz's passing. She expected to feel deeply moved when she saw it, but it was home that she longed for: these walls, this marble under foot. Riad Bovary was her mausoleum, the spectacular resting place of her great love, her only love. There was nothing else that could come close.

On the bus back to Delhi, she had closed her eyes against the heat and listened to two young women talking in English. The one sighed and said, can you imagine someone loving you enough to do all that? The other replied, hell, I'd settle for a bloody second date. Monique wanted to interrupt them, to say, no, it's true, such love exists in the world! I have known it. She wanted to touch the taut skin of their faces and look into their bright eyes and see all the lives that were yet to unfold. She said nothing, only put her hand into her pocket and rubbed her thumb against the hard smooth baby secreted inside.

She was twenty-one when she came to Morocco. A girl, practically a child. It was on her father's insistence that she visit, he wanted her to sleep under the stars of the great Sahara, a rite of passage he had shared with his father and one he had dreamed about enjoying with his own son. But Eduard was dead and buried, and a daughter was all he had left. Claude, her father, fancied himself an adventurer. He had joined de Gaulle's Free French forces during the war, led troops through North Africa, and in the process fallen hopelessly in love with the continent all over again, with the endless expanse of sky and sand and the humbleness of the people, who appeared to him both regal and in possession of some arcane wisdom and grace. After the war, he returned to France with great reluctance. He was already married, his wife had suffered enough with his absence during the war, she would not consent to further marital sacrifice and a life spent living out her husband's colonial fantasies. They rented a tiny apartment in Paris, a room really, with a little stove and a bathroom down the hall shared by everyone on their floor. It felt like prison to Claude, cramped and airless and achingly dull. He contemplated running away and once almost did, but then his wife opened her bathrobe one morning and showed him the bump that was forming.

In Marrakech, Claude had guided his daughter through the rabbit warren of the medina, past the carpet sellers and herbalists and the men sitting street side drinking pots of mint tea and arguing about the world. He knocked on the tiny wooden door of a crumbling house and, when it opened, ushered her inside a magnificent riad that smelled of saffron and lemons. The owner of the house was Omar, onetime soldier and longtime friend of Claude's. The two men greeted each other with kisses on the cheek. Omar summoned his children and grandchildren from the other rooms and as the two families smiled and kissed, Monique was struck by the man her father appeared to be in this faraway place. It was Friday, Omar's wife had prepared couscous with lamb and vegetables. She presented the food on a dish so large it required her two sons to carry it. They sat upon cushions on the floor around a low table.

Eat, eat, Omar urged, and she watched her father stick his hands into the food and scoop out a handful of warm couscous. He shoved his fingers into his mouth, licked the fat, and declared it delicious. The rest of the family put their hands into the dish, ate hungrily. Try it, Claude instructed his daughter, go on. She put a few fingers into the food, gingerly scooped some up, and put it into her mouth. It was the best thing she had ever tasted. She smiled, she ate more; her father gave her knee a pat.

Good girl, he said, that's it, and she felt he had never been prouder.

In Paris she had a boyfriend, a sweet but dull man who loved her a little too much. She expected that he would propose soon enough and she would be obliged to say yes. The idea filled her with mild dread but she hid it well. Her mother was terribly excited about the prospect of a son-in-law who was a lawyer. Claude took her to Volubilis, to the ancient Roman ruins, they visited Fez and stayed in a riad that had once belonged to the philosopher Aziz Lahbabi. They got lost in the medina's elbow-wide alleyways, paid children to lead them back to where they came from. In the markets, they sampled dates and pastries heavy with honey and orange blossom, they ate tagines cooked for hours over coals piled onto little corners of the street, and never refused the offer of a mint tea with a curious stranger. Everywhere, Claude spoke Arabic like it was his mother tongue. Monique was struck by how easily her father fit into this world, as though it was here that he belonged all along.

You're so happy here, she remarked, and he nodded sadly.

From Erfoud, they headed into the Erg Chebbi desert, guided by Addi, a six-foot Tuareg man with a wide smile and green eyes. He had brought two camels, one for Claude and one for her. He would be on foot, and shoeless. The camels were not easy to ride over the dunes, their spindly legs seemed to give way from time to time as they struggled downhill. Monique held tight to the metal handle, felt her muscles tense and relax as she tried to move in rhythm with the animal.

You're doing splendidly, Claude called to her.

Yes, yes, Addi agreed, your daughter is very good Berber!

The animals were flatulent and uncomfortable, but the desert—the silence and the vastness and the feeling of being alone in the world—it was magic. The first day they trekked eight or so hours, stopping only briefly for a modest lunch of nuts and fruit prepared by Addi. After lunch they continued on until they reached a small Berber compound.

We will rest here tonight, Addi said, and he helped them off the camels.

They ate a meal of vegetables and chicken, cooked in a tagine buried in the sand since the morning. The chicken's head and feet sat in the dish, pale and fatty. As the sun began to set the sky turned pink and then orange and then black. It was the most beautiful thing Monique had ever witnessed. They sat under the stars, father and daughter, silent and content. A Berber woman covered head to toe in robes and scarves ushered them into a tent laid out with carpets to sleep upon.

It's safe, Addi said. Berber carpets dyed with saffron to keep away the snakes!

They slept deeply and in the morning set off once again, this time with a different guide. I am Bakai, the man said.

He spoke to them in perfect French, inquired about their night and if their dinner had been satisfactory. He had gleaming white teeth and eyes dark like onyx.

Are you also Tuareg? Monique asked.

No, madame, he replied. I am a nomad.

Bakai, in his blue djellaba, also walked barefoot.

Is the sand not hot? Monique asked.

He smiled, I am used to it, he replied. It is easier for me to walk without shoes.

Claude that day seemed to be in a slight decline, perhaps too many regrets or memories at the surface. He spoke little, and rode off at a distance. Monique and Bakai had hours to talk. By the time they reached that night's Berber camp, it had already transpired: Monique was in love. She loved the way Bakai moved, his muscles neat and perfect under the robes; she loved how he spoke, his voice deep and soft at the same time, liquid almost. He took care with her, held her hand as she dismounted the camel, offered her water and tea and looked into her eyes and through to the other side; she could hardly breathe with his gaze upon her.

That night, as her father snored in the tent, she lifted the blankets off her and slipped outside into the cool desert air. The stars were out, lighting her way as she walked softly with the sand underfoot. The camels were tethered together, each one with a hind leg bound to prevent it wandering off. It was heady, the night and the stars and the smallness of everything but the sky. She headed slowly toward the dune, felt her heart pump with blood as she climbed to the top. Looking down, she could see the tents and the camels, tiny dots in a sea of sand, a microcosm of life as opposite to her own as one could get. You are alright, madame? It was Bakai, he had followed her up the dune, as she had hoped.

Oh yes, she said. I think I have never been better.

How strange the life that finds you, the life that snatches you from everything you know to be true and holds you fast and firm in its grip, refusing to let go. She did not return to France with her father, or with her mother, who made a special trip out to Morocco to try to persuade her daughter of the lunacy of her decision.

I will never return, she declared.

Bakai it turned out was married already, with several children and one on the way. He could offer her nothing more than a few stolen days every few months, between time in the desert and time with his family. Still, it was enough, anything was enough; those hours together sacred and exquisite. She moved to Fez, rented a little room with a family but soon realized that she would need privacy in order to avoid scandal. She wrote to her father and begged him for a loan. She implored him to understand her decision, to allow her to honor her great love.

I suspect your life was not in the end the life of your choosing, she wrote, *I believe that when we fight our destiny we die a little more each day, until one day nothing is left but the negative space once occupied by dreams. Please Father,* she wrote, *please help me.* He wired her the money the following week, enough to buy the riad and a little left over to fix it up. She called it Riad Bovary to be ironic, and maybe a little dramatic, but it suited her nonetheless and she settled into her new life with remarkable ease. Madame Monique, the locals called her, always a little awed by the young French girl who lived alone in a faraway place.

You have no husband? the women asked, and when she replied that she did not, they shook their heads and speculated among themselves what the reason for such misfortune might be.

Bakai visited when he could, always knocking on the door and inquiring at the desk if he might book a room for the night. She would smile calmly while her heart beat furiously and her body braced itself for the long-awaited thrill of his touch.

Yes sir, she'd say, we would be delighted to accommodate you for the evening.

He would have no bag, no change of clothing, only a stash of fresh dates wrapped in brown paper brought for her from the desert as a gift. She would have one of the staff escort him upstairs—always to the same room—and spend the hours until evening trying not to blush. After finishing up for the night, she would head upstairs, slip into her own room to change her underwear and brush her teeth, and then knock softly on the door next to hers.

My beautiful, he would say, opening up, leading her inside where they would lie entwined in each other's arms.

In the morning she would find him on the floor, curled into the carpet because the bed was too soft. She always asked after his family and he always told her with pride about his sons, who were strong, and his daughters, who were becoming beautiful. She did not feel jealousy toward them, only some strange sense of kinship: they loved the same man, they were one family.

When her father died suddenly, she returned for a brief time to France. Her mother was old with grief, lined and brittle as if she might break.

You must come home now, she said, we are all that is left.

She helped her mother pack up the closets and bundled up her father's shirts and books into cardboard boxes. He had surprisingly little, for a man of so many years. In the back of the wardrobe she found his journals from his time in the war and slipped them into her coat to take with her.

I think I will die soon too, her mother said, we are not meant to exist in solitude.

Perhaps you will come to Fez, Monique said. The change would do you good.

Her mother sneered, lit a cigarette, and said with bitterness, you are just like him, happiest when farthest away from me.

Monique left after several weeks, exhausted from tending to her mother's need and from her own grief at being fatherless. But also there was something else.

In Fez, the doctor examined her and frowned.

You are some weeks along, he said.

He regarded her coldly, prodded her belly with rough fingers that gave her gooseflesh. The nurse looked on uncomfortably. They were aware that she was unmarried. There was no way of getting the news to Bakai, she could only wait until his next visit, and there was no knowing when that might be. She sat sipping tea in the kitchen of the riad, hands trembling with a mix of dread and delight. A child, her child, their child. She knew there would be difficulties, disapproval.

She started to show some months later, a rounding of her belly which no one was shy to point out.

You are getting so fat! the women at the market declared, laughing.

Yes, she smiled, I am having a baby.

One of the women said something to her friend, and both women shook their heads. Faizel, who worked in the kitchen, came to her one afternoon to tell her that he was leaving.

You bring shame upon yourself, he scowled, and shame on me if I work for you.

Soon after, the others left too. They needed the money but not at the cost of their moral standing in the community. It was too great a scandal. Monique sent a telegram to her mother, asked her to come to Fez for the birth. The reply was curt, not altogether unexpected.

I have no daughter, her mother wrote.

She signed with her Christian name, not Mother, as she had always done.

Still, Monique did not feel alone those months. She felt the hardness of her belly, the sharp pain that told her life grew there, slow and steady. She made a quilt and found a man who would build her a crib. She did not mind taking over the cleaning of the rooms and the cooking of the guests' breakfasts; she found the labor somehow beautiful, an ode to the new life she was creating. She watched as her body changed in the mirror and imagined how it would please Bakai to see her fill out. She wrote out names for boys and girls, in Arabic and in French. If it was a boy she would name him after her father.

One day at the door there stood a man.

Madame, he said in French, I believe you are short of staff.

Yes, she smiled, it seems that Riad Bovary is not an altogether desirable place to work. She indicated her belly. It is a little scandalous, she said.

Beneath the man's djellaba she saw that he was skin over bone. He smiled at her. Perhaps we can be helpful to one another, he said.

His name was Hassan, he had crossed over from Algeria on foot. Monique hired him on the spot, sat him down at the kitchen table, and made him eat a breakfast of yogurt and eggs and oranges.

At twenty weeks she was brought to her knees. The pain was unbearable. She ordered a taxi to deliver her to the hospital. The doctor on duty slipped on a plastic glove and opened her up with his hand.

Something is wrong, he said. We will do more tests.

They took blood and urine and another doctor put on another plastic glove and felt her insides. She curled into a ball and wept, for pain and loneliness and the terror of everything unknown. They gave her painkillers, which allowed her to sleep. When she woke the doctor told her she would need an operation.

We need to remove the baby, he said.

No, she cried, you cannot take my child.

I am sorry, he said, but there is no child. Only stone.

It was called lithopedion, she learned later, the calcification of a fetus that dies during an abdominal pregnancy. A doomed child in the wrong place, suspended in time and turned into stone. She allowed the doctor to remove it on condition that he keep the baby to give to her afterward. He looked at her sadly but agreed. As the anesthetic took effect, she had a vision of herself in the Sahara, lying on the hot sand and cradling a stone. The sun beat down on her and the wind shifted the dunes until they buried her completely under sand. I am drowning, she mumbled, and then all was dark. She woke sore and in a haze. There were nurses around her speaking quietly in Arabic. She could tell that they were talking about her, motioning at her belly and at something beside her bed. She tried to make out the words but fell once more into the quiet of sleep. Later, she saw it too. The baby in a jar beside her bed. Stone baby. Her baby. It was the size of a golf ball, the color of sand. She opened the lid of the jar and removed it. In her belly the pain was severe. She welcomed it, breathed into the wound and gripped her fingers around the rock-hard child in her palm. The tears she couldn't stop, and so she let them come. The nurse came up to her and touched her gently on the head.

The pain will pass in time, madame, she said.

Monique clutched the baby and brought it to her lips to kiss. Already she loved it and would forever.

The doctor came the next day with a solemn face. There were some complications, he said. I am terribly sorry.

The baby had been too deeply lodged to her insides, there was no way to remove it without taking the uterus. There would be no more children. Only the child of stone.

Is there someone I may call to collect you? the doctor inquired, and it was Hassan's name she gave.

Back at the riad, he tended to her with great care. He brought her meals to her room and insisted on sleeping outside the door so that she could call for him in the night. She showed him the stone baby, and he held it with fascination and tenderness.

Is it a boy or a girl, he asked, and she realized that she had no idea.

It was some weeks later that Bakai appeared back at the riad. He held her in his arms as she told him of the pregnancy and the baby and the fact that she would never bear more of his children.

You are well, he said, you are here, this is what matters.

He held the baby, traced with his finger the outline of head and torso. It is a miracle, he said.

Why? she asked.

He kissed her lips and put the stone into her palm. This child we made will live a million million years. It cannot die, it cannot turn to dust.

Because the riad was empty of guests and because Hassan was

Hassan, the three of them sat together and ate dinner around the table.

Hassan has been my savior, she told Bakai.

And madame mine, Hassan replied.

Bakai took Hassan by the hand and kissed him on each cheek. Then it is good we have found each other in this world, he said.

Before Bakai left again for the Sahara, he presented Monique with a gift. It was something he'd had made for her, a little pouch embroidered with gold thread that she could wear around her waist.

So you can keep the baby close, he said. He tied it gently around her and she slipped the baby inside.

It was hard sometimes to remember those years, the tremendous longing between visits with Bakai, the elation when he would arrive at the door at last. In bad seasons, he would come only once in the year, and she would read on his face the shame and the disappointment as he stood before her.

I could lend you a little money, she offered once and never again.

It had been the cause of their first and only argument. He would never consent to taking her money. There were times when loneliness gave way to despair, when the gaze of a man on the street reminded her of everything she was missing out on. There was an American diplomat who stayed at the riad for three weeks. He asked her to prepare him dinner on a few occasions, and then insisted that she join him in eating it.

So, he said, you must be running from something or toward someone. Which is it?

After dinner he pressed his lips against hers and put his hand under her shirt. You are disarmingly beautiful, he said.

She let herself follow him upstairs and in the morning washed the stains of him from her skin. There were others, always only brief and sweet. Love was reserved for Bakai alone.

The guests at the riad were often incredulous.

But you live here, they said, all alone?

Yes, she would reply, and there is nowhere else I would want to be. It was almost true.

She read books, she learned Arabic, she busied herself with the endless restoration of the riad.

Why do you do this? Hassan asked.

She smiled, because I would like to leave something behind when I die, something perfect and beautiful.

Any money she made from the tourists she poured into the restoration, there was always something more to be done. Years when there was a little left over, she would book a flight somewhere far away. Cambodia, India, Brazil, Turkey, Jordan. She loved the smells and the colors and the food, she loved leaving and she loved the return. There was Hassan too, of course, her constant companion, her most loyal friend.

Hassan, she often said, what would have become of us if you had not found your way to my door?

He too had no family, no home but this one. There had been only one conversation between them about his life before Fez, but she could guess at the circumstances of his departure from Algeria, his lack of family ties, his disinterest in finding a wife. They made a perfect match.

Years became decades. She watched her youth leave her, slowly at first and then all at once. She was now an old woman, not yet frail, but not far from it either. Her hair was gray, her face lined with everything that had passed. Still, Bakai called her beautiful, still he kissed her with tenderness and desire. He was old too, worn by time and sun. On recent visits, she had noticed how he breathed at night, almost a struggle. She wondered how many more crossings of the Sahara he would be able to make before his legs gave way. He told her that his youngest son was almost ready to take over from him and she was glad. His wife was ill, he said, he needed to look after her. Monique, despite herself, felt a flicker of hope. If his wife died, it might be possible for him to spend more time with her in Fez.

She walked quickly now through the narrow warren of the medina, the houses in some places so close that it was hard to pass at all. After all these years she could make her way on instinct alone, finding her way effortlessly through the old town, through the vendors and the hordes of tourists on their way to the tanneries, through the winding markets past the odd donkey laden with goods to sell. At the market she waited while the man sliced wedges of flaky pancakes and wrapped them in paper for her breakfast guests. She spoke to him in Arabic, made him laugh, and felt as always the pleasure of such an exchange. From the fruit seller she bought kiwis and oranges, she sent wishes to his wife, who was having their fifth baby, and made her way back to the riad. As she opened the door, Hassan came to her.

Someone is here to see you, he said. His face was grave.

Who is it? she asked.

He took the shopping from her and pointed her to the study. He is in there.

It was a young man, and he rose as she entered the room. He wore a blue djellaba, a nomad or a Berber, she thought. She greeted him in Arabic, which made him smile. As he did, she recognized him. It could only be him.

You are a son of Bakai, she said. She sank into the sofa.

In French, he replied. Yes, I am Bakar. And you are Madame Monique.

Hassan without a word laid a tray of tea on the table and then left the room.

Bakar, Monique said. I have heard about you from your father. You look very much like him.

Bakar nodded. Yes, all my father's sons do.

Madame Monique, he said, please forgive my intrusion of your home, I am—

Please, Bakar, Monique interrupted, tell me why you have come. Is your father ill?

Bakar shook his head. No, madame, he said. He is not ill. He has already passed. Monique heard the words but shook her head. No, no, it is not possible, she said. It cannot be so.

Her head spun, her heart a tremendous pounding she could feel in her ears. She put a hand in her pocket and squeezed, felt the cold and hard stone against her flesh. She looked at Bakar, at the face staring back at her, familiar and strange at the same time. Bakai's son, Bakai's son.

I am sorry, he said. I am sorry to bear this news.

Monique clasped a hand over her mouth, shut her eyes against the tears. Is it possible, she said, is it possible I will never see him again?

Bakar shifted in his seat; she remembered suddenly that she was not the only grief-stricken woman he would have had to break the news to.

I'm sorry, Monique said, composing herself. It is a great loss for your family. For your mother.

Bakar opened his hands to the sky. It is God's will, he said. He had a good life. Many children. He knew great love. These are things to make a man happy. He cannot ask for more.

Monique nodded. He was very proud of you, she said. I can see why.

Bakar motioned toward the tea on the table. May I take something to drink, he asked. My goodness, she said, of course. You have walked, from the desert?

Most of the journey, Bakar said.

It was kind of you to come, she said. You have done an old woman a great kindness.

Bakar drank his tea and she filled his glass again. My father told me about you some years ago, he said. He spoke of his love for a Frenchwoman in Fez, Madame Monique from Riad Bovary. He would have wanted you to be informed.

Monique shifted. You must think I am an awful woman, she said.

Bakar shook his head. No, madame, not at all. I think you are a courageous woman. You followed the calling of your heart.

Yes, she said quietly. And now that heart is broken.

You must be hungry, she said suddenly. I would like to prepare you some food. And offer you a room to stay the night. Please, she said.

Let me return your kindness.

Bakar nodded, that would be very welcome, he said.

She showed him to a room and went to the kitchen. Hassan, standing over a pot, held out his arms to her. She wept on his shoulder and he stroked her hair. Together they cooked a stew of chicken and vegetables, Hassan made bread and sliced up some cake left over from the breakfast guests.

Monique went to summon Bakar to lunch, but found him already asleep in the room, flat on his back on the floor. Downstairs, the Englishman was waiting with his backpack at the entrance.

You are going today? Monique asked, struggling to remember who was due to leave or arrive.

For three nights, yes, the man said. The Path of Love and Presence. In the Middle Atlas?

Yes, yes, Monique said. Mr. Tom. Of course, you are participating in the retreat. And you will be back afterward. I am sorry, she said, waving a hand in the air. Everything is everywhere today.

He smiled at her. But perhaps everything is just where it should be, he said.

They ate together later that night, Monique and Bakar, and the next five nights after that. Monique found him to be much like his father, his gestures, his voice, the way he spoke with his eyes.

What will you do now? she asked.

Bakar set down his tea. I will take over from my father, he said. As a Sahara guide.

Do you enjoy it? Monique asked.

Oh yes, he said. I am under the stars every night, all around me there is sky and space. This is everything I need for my happiness.

Monique nodded sadly, yes, she said, that is what your father said too.

And what will you do? he asked. Will you return home?

Oh, she laughed. This is the only home I have known.

There were some things of Bakai's that had gathered in the riad over the years, shoes and books. Monique bundled them up and gave them to Bakar.

We had a child, she said. I suppose you would have been an older brother. She showed the baby to Bakar and he turned the stone over in his hands.

It is a good reminder, he said.

Of what, she asked.

That life is strange, he said, and beautiful in its strangeness.

When he left, Monique handed him two things. An envelope of all the dirhams she had in the world, and a small pouch with a stone inside.

WE BELONG NOWHERE
BUT OURSELVES

Bakar said it was the sand that broke the news first. The shifting directions, the way nothing was the same as the years before and the years before that. The sand tells more truth than a man ever will, is what he says. He learned that from his father. He learned everything from his father. He says everything in the world can be traced back to a pattern in the dunes and the feel of a single grain of sand on your tongue. When we started out, he gave me a few grains to put under my tongue.

Feel, he said.

It feels like sand in my mouth, I replied and he laughed.

Yes, that is exactly correct, he said, you are a clever girl.

I like Bakar, I like him so much I wish I never had to leave him but I know that's not how this works.

I'm fifteen but really mature for my age. You mature quickly during times of crises, that's what I've heard. In which case I guess all the kids across the world are pretty mature these days. And not really kids any longer. It's a shame how things are, how the world kind of fell apart in a few years, a domino effect that destroyed everything pretty much everywhere but here. My mother had been predicting it for years. She was really smart. She told me what was coming. She told me how it would be.

Out here, you'd think everything was just fine in the world. It's so quiet, so peaceful. So few people. Actually, almost none at all. We came upon another Berber guide three days ago but since then it's been just us. Me, Bakar, and Tilda. I like it, the quiet and the calm. None of the chaos of before, when everyone was screaming in the streets or ready to kill you for a tin of cat food. I like not seeing the news on TV, always more tragedy, always more bad news. Sometimes it feels like a movie I watched, like it all happened to someone else or not at all. Then I think of my mother.

We spend most days sitting around in the sand or trying to sleep. We make a little fire and cook something if we've been lucky enough to find provisions or we just pass around the nuts and dates and dried apricots from the stash Bakar keeps tied to Julep, our camel.

Good for your diets, ladies, Bakar likes to joke.

I don't think Tilda finds it funny but she laughs anyway and eats what's in front of her. We're skin over bone, but used to being hungry. My mother used to say you can get used to pretty much anything. All it takes is repetition and then something that was strange before becomes normal. I think about everything that's happened and she was right. This is the new normal.

You can't not like Bakar. He's the best person in the world. We walk at night, all night, because it's cooler and also because it's easier to stay out of sight of the desert police. If they find you they're meant to kill you on the spot, no trial, no chance to explain your way out of it. This is the law now. I guess it makes sense. I guess it's the only way to stop the whole world from coming here and taking what's left. Divine retribution for colonization, is what Tilda said a few nights ago, whatever that means. She's German but her accent sounds British. She has really pale skin and she keeps her head wrapped in a scarf all day to keep from blistering under the sun.

Tilda and I take turns riding Julep. She'll take a few hours and then we'll switch. Bakar never rides Julep. He says he prefers to walk. He goes barefoot too, because he says shoes make it too hard for him to walk in the sand. He never had one day in school but Bakar is the smartest man I've ever met. He can speak seven languages, just like that. He knows about the stars and the planets and the history of the world and even stuff like philosophy and poetry. My mother would have liked him a lot, I know it. To tell the truth, I wish it were Bakar who was my father. Or I wish he liked me so much he'd decide to adopt me. We could stay together always and he could teach me about the desert and I'd learn to speak Arabic and French and Berber like he does. I wish it every day even though I know it's not going to come true. Some things just can't be made real no matter how much you want them to.

My real father is the person I'm going to find. Or at least that's the plan. The only plan. We should have a plan B, I told my mother when we talked about us leaving. Oh no, she said, we only need a really good plan A, and this is it. She was strong, my mother, like a warrior, but still when the illness came it floored her and we knew what was coming next.

I'm sorry, she kept saying, I'm so sorry to leave you like this.

I held her head in my lap and wiped her forehead with a cool cloth. I told her that I would be okay, that I'd make it across without her and that I'd find a way to stay alive. Inside I was thinking maybe I didn't mind dying so much myself. In some ways it seemed like the easier thing to do because why would you want to be the only one alive when everyone else you love in the world is dead? It was weird then because I think my mother read my thoughts right out of my head. She had a way of doing that sometimes. Anyway, she sat right up and held my face in her hands.

Promise me, Zaria, she said. Promise me you are not going to die here, not like this. You have to try. You have to go.

Mothers on their deathbed are not people you can say no to. I kissed her, one on each cheek and one on the lips, and said, yes Mom, I promise.

And now I'm here.

I'm not very good at this, am I? I didn't even start at the beginning but it's hard to remember everything at once and put it down in the right order. The year is 2031. My name is Zaria Morgan. I am fifteen years old. I am crossing the Sahara Desert with Bakar, the

Berber guide, and Tilda (last name unknown). I am making my way south to find my father. His name is Kingdom. His last name is unknown too.

Sometimes I forget exactly how it all started, how I ended up with a dead mother and a pretty treacherous plan A to execute all on my own. Life seemed to be mostly normal when I was growing up and then suddenly it wasn't and there was no going back. No more pancake Sundays with my mother, no more taking the bikes to Vondelpark to lie on blankets in the sun. No more school. No more holidays in France. The news on TV was bad for a while, and then it was always bad with no good bits in between. There were the floods, the torrential rains that went on for weeks and weeks and sent whole villages floating away. Hurricanes and tsunamis, tornadoes and landslides and ferocious storms; everything like in a movie but it was all real and there was no ending to wrap it all up and let you go back to normal. Then came the droughts, the crop failures in the Northern Hemisphere and food shortages across Asia, the Americas, and Europe. The farmlands turned to dust bowls, nothing growing, nothing with any life left to give. The weekly markets closed, there wasn't produce for anyone to sell. We bought our food in tins from the supermarkets, and then when the government started rationing things, we'd queue up outside the mosque to collect the weekly quota. At first the queuing was kind of fun. We'd run into the neighbors and my mother would chat to them and they'd laugh about government hysteria and give an opinion on how long they thought it would last. But then after a while you could tell it was going to last a long time, and maybe forever. The weather wasn't something anyone could control or fix. The disasters were happening too fast and too frequently for anyone to pick up the pieces.

On the news you'd see footage that looked familiar, thousands of people piling up their belongings and heading off to start a new life. But it wasn't war driving them away this time. They called them the environmental refugees and every day there were more of them, huddled together like sheep trying to keep warm in a storm. People headed south before they realized that south wasn't any better off. It was the same everywhere, one giant disaster that couldn't be contained or escaped; the world imploding. They called it the Era of Collapse. They had scientists on talk shows shaking their heads and pointing to maps covered in red or blue: red for drought, blue for flood.

No one listened, they said, no one thought it would happen this soon.

People didn't smile in the food queues anymore. The neighbors didn't chat, they looked at what everyone else had in their boxes and shouted if they didn't get the same. When the riots and looting started, you could only go out during curfew. The police were everywhere, keeping things in order even though most of them looked too tired and hungry to lift their weapons even if they needed to.

Sometimes on the streets you'd hear the doomsday preachers talking about the end of the world, and for the first time no one thought they were crazy. It felt like it was happening for real. People were always hungry, always cold. They got sick a lot. Everything stopped working, offices shut, stores closed their doors. Money didn't mean anything anymore, not a thing, because what people needed could no longer be bought. When the Great Food War of 2025 broke out, we had no food for weeks. A lot of people died. You'd see their bodies being carted off, some of them without so much as a sheet to cover them up. Old people, babies, kids I'd played with on our street. My mother would hold a hand over my eyes so I wouldn't have to see the corpses but eventually there was no hiding from it.

Are we going to die too? I asked.

She bit her lip and shook her head. No, she said, no we are not.

On the news we'd see scenes from other countries—bushfires, floods, farmlands standing barren and bare.

Jesus, my mother said, the apocalypse is here.

The epidemics came next, diseases wiping out hundreds of thousands of people at a time. The refugees kept packing up and moving on, even though there was nowhere decent left to go. I guess it made people feel better about things if they at least tried.

There were a lot of suicides, people who didn't want to face what was happening, what was ahead. A lot of families did it together, overdosed or drank poison. You knew sometimes it was going to happen, because there'd be a knock at the door and you'd open up to find a box of provisions left for you to use. We cried a lot, my mother and I. There were so many people we lost, people who took their own lives or just faded away to nothing. Our neighbors the Soeters came to the door one evening, all five of them lined up together. Marie was wiping tears from her eyes, holding tightly to the baby who was not even a year old.

We can't anymore, she said.

My mother kissed them all one by one, hugged them close, and touched her hand to their faces like she was committing them to memory.

There's not much to take, Marie said, but you help yourselves to whatever can be useful. She pressed a little pouch into my mother's hands. Don't need jewelry in the next life, she said.

My mother closed the door when they left and sank to the floor. I sat beside her and wondered when she would suggest that we do it too. I think I hoped she would.

In all the chaos in all the world, somehow most of Africa was spared. There were no droughts or floods, the crops still grew, the cities weren't all underwater like the rest of the world. At first, the governments there made deals with the rest of the world. They sent over food and supplies, then they started accepting refugees. If you had money, you could get out. You'd see homes in the best neighborhoods with the front door open and the inside cleared out, not a soul left. They left their pets most of the time, you'd see dogs sitting guard at the door of an empty house.

It didn't take long before the leaders of the African Union realized that all the money in the world would be pretty pointless in the long term if the whole world collapsed. So they closed their borders, and stopped the flights. You could get out, but you couldn't get in, no matter how much money you had. We were all just stuck, waiting to run out of food or die from disease or get washed away in a flood. No one was going to save us. No one could even save themselves.

That's when the exit centers sprang up. You could walk in and they'd ask you some questions and if you chose to die, they'd show you to a special room with nice couches and paintings of the sea on the walls. They would lay you down and give you an injection and you could close your eyes and fade away. GO IN PEACE! the posters said. Some people thought it was just the government trying to make their resources stretch further, but I think most folks were grateful to have a way out. You'd walk past some days and the queue would be all the way around the block.

You heard a lot of rumors then, some of them true or half-true. One rumor was about a way out; the only way left. When we came up with plan A we didn't care about it being real or not, we just cared about taking one last shot at surviving. The story was that you had to get as far south as you could, into Spain and then all the way down to Tarifa. They'd closed the borders of course but there was an underground network that could get you across by boat into Morocco. From there, you went south, making your way down to the desert and then crossing the Sahara with the Berbers or nomads who were willing to guide you in exchange for gold or stones.

We'll do it, my mother said.

We had the jewelry from Marie and some bits and pieces my mother hadn't yet sold on the black market in the early days of the rations. We took the atlas down off the shelf and spent hours looking at maps, charting a route from Holland to Spain. We looked at the photographs of Morocco, of the desert at night with the stars and nothing else in the blackness.

We'll do it, Zaria, my mother said. We'll make it across the desert and then we'll keep going south. Her eyes went shiny and she looked far, far away. We'll go to South Africa, she said. We'll go find your father.

I'd known about my father since I was a little girl. Or, at least, I knew everything there was to know about him, which wasn't very much at all. I knew he was from somewhere in Africa and that my mother had met him on a trip she took to Cape Town when she was young. I knew that she had wanted to get pregnant, that she'd had some kind of epiphany where she saw herself with a baby girl the color of caramel. She didn't mind raising me alone, she said, she didn't mind never seeing my father again. She told me that everything that had happened since the night I was conceived unfolded like a story she'd read a long time ago.

Zaria, she always said, you are everything I ever needed to do with my life.

I never missed having a father before, but I started to like the idea of us going to find him in Africa. My mother had a photograph of the two of them together, the only one we had in the whole house. She'd given it to me when I was just a little girl and I had kept it in a frame beside my bed. I liked his name, which made him sound really important, and I liked to imagine that when he saw us he'd be excited and happy and relieved that we were alive. This is your daughter, my mother would say, and he'd look me up and down and smile because I'd be part him and part her. They might fall in love again, or maybe not, but it wouldn't matter anyway because my mother always said that love was transient and shouldn't be measured in time but in the way it transforms you. She'd had a lot of boyfriends over the years and she loved them all.

When most of the people around us were preparing to die, my mother and I started preparing to leave. We'd go out foraging for food, creeping into abandoned apartments and searching the cupboards for tins or dried goods. Most of what was edible was already gone, but sometimes you'd still get lucky or stumble upon someone's underground cellar. We always waited two days, one day scouting the place and one day afterward just to make sure no one was coming home. It was always a strange feeling, walking through the rooms of other people's lives. And most likely, deaths. Once we found a man in his basement, hanging from his belt in the dark. A few times I saw my mother slip something into her pockets, jewelry or watches. It's not stealing if there's no one around to claim it, she'd say, and I would nod. The rules had changed. Good people did bad things when they had to. As our stash grew and our plan took shape we started feeling hopeful, even excited. It seemed like there was a chance it could work, that we'd find a way. We started saying things like, when we get to Cape Town, we'll go for a swim in the sea, or, when we're in the desert we'll need to learn to ride a camel. I guess I ought to have felt bad that we were going to survive and other people weren't, but by then it was really just my mother and me left anyway. Two peas in our pod, she always said.

Then she got ill. It came quickly, one night she was fine and the next morning she was the color of death. There were no doctors, no medicine. We both knew there was no getting better. She had a fever and before long it was in her lungs, her breathing slow and painful. The death rattle, is what they call it. I looked it up in the medical journal she'd inherited from her grandfather. I tried so hard not to cry in front of her. Inside it was like someone was twisting a knife in me. We made promises to each other, she and I. We went over the plan. She wrote everything down in a notebook while she still could and then when she couldn't anymore, she spoke and I wrote. Dates and names and borders and things to remember. We called it Zaria's Great Adventure so it sounded like something exciting rather than what it was, a do or die situation.

You need to go, she said one morning. I don't want you here to watch me die.

No, I said, I am staying here until the end.

I got under the blankets with her to keep her warm. Her body felt like ice on my skin and I shivered. In the morning, I found a bag packed with our food and some blankets and the pouch of jewelry. My mother next to me was not breathing. I was alone in the world.

I could have found a way to end everything that morning, to slip sweetly away without any more heartache, without being witness to any more of the sadness in the world. I don't even know for sure why I didn't. I guess something in me wanted to fight after all. I kissed my mother and she already felt cold and small, not like a person who had lived but a mannequin of a woman. I wrapped her up in the blanket and put a photograph of the two of us in her hands. It was a picture we'd taken on our last trip to France, the two of us in a field of wildflowers, squinting into the camera and squeezing our faces together so close that it looked like two halves of the same person. I took the bag, looked around our apartment one last time, and then closed the door behind me.

It was strangers along the way who were the kindest, maybe because I was all alone or maybe because no one believed I'd ever really get to where I said I was going. Most people were quiet and frightened, waiting for the inevitable. Everyone seemed lonely, even if they were not alone. When I told them my mother was gone, they would cry and hug me, and I could tell that their tears were not only for me, but for us all. I slept in bunkers and storm shelters and sometimes just in apartments where the owners had long since died or departed. I walked through the rooms, looking at photographs and bookshelves and crockery, trying to imagine the ordinariness of people's lives before the future got rewritten. There was no trouble in Spain, the authorities had stopped bothering to keep people in when there was almost no hope of them getting out anyway. The cities I walked through were ruins, unrecognizable as places that once buzzed with life and people. I remembered how my mother had shown me Roman ruins in a book, long before the catastrophes began.

The history of the world, she said. Build, break, then build again. Because life is a circle, not a line.

I wondered who would be around to rebuild things this time, the ones who would unearth the ruins.

Along the way I kept the map close and the notebook hidden inside my shirt. My mother had put her copy of *Moby-Dick* in the bag too, one of the few books I hadn't yet read. *Zaria*, she'd written inside it. *Zaria, my light, my heart. Be brave, beautiful child. I know you will find your way. I know you will be strong. I know you will survive.* These are the last words I'll ever have of hers, the last things she wanted to say to me. I don't know how many times I've read them since I left, maybe a hundred or more. I read the inscription every day, a ritual like brushing my teeth, which actually we do here using a piece of twig from a tree.

I won't talk about everything, because some of the things that have happened along the way are not parts I want to think about, or even put into words. Let's just say not all people are good people. I think Tilda must know about that stuff too, because sometimes I catch her staring off into nowhere, her face a blank, her eyes shut off like she refuses to see one more bad thing in her lifetime.

I'm not a talker, she said the first day when I asked her a lot of questions, like where was she from and did she have kids and where was she going.

Now I wait till she says something to me before talking to her. Some days we don't even say a word, it's only me and Bakar whose voices you can hear. It's a funny thing, being with someone every day and knowing that they will always be a stranger. I watch her and try to guess things sometimes. Like how did she learn to light a fire from sticks, and why is she fluent in Arabic and what happened to the finger on her left hand that isn't there.

She did ask me once about my mother. I showed her the note she wrote me in my book and she read it and then said, your mother must have loved you very much.

She turned away and I could see her biting down on her lip and digging the nail of one hand into the flesh of the other. Another time she asked me where I was headed.

Cape Town, I said, to my father.

She looked surprised when I said I'd never met him or spoken to him before. She asked me what I was going to do if I couldn't find him and I don't know why but I burst into tears.

I don't know, I shouted, I don't know what I'll do!

Tilda apologized very quietly and let me ride Julep the rest of that night. In the dark where no one could tell, I let the tears wash me like the sea.

I think my mother would have loved it in the desert. She loved nothing better than space and sky, no walls closing you in, no ceilings bearing down on you.

Zaria, she told me, when you see an African sunset for the first time, you'll realize how small we are in the world, how we are nothing but a speck in time.

She was right. The first night in the desert I almost wept. The colors, painted in blues and pinks against the sky, the perfect circle of the moon sitting high above and indifferent to everything below it. I wished my mother were with me. I tried to tell myself that she was.

Bakar asked me when we first met where I came from.

Holland, I told him. My mother was Dutch.

And your father? he asked me, because your skin is like mine.

Oh, I said, he was from Africa.

Bakar smiled and held up his hands. Then you are going home, he said.

I liked that idea very much. Having a father, having a home even though I'd only ever seen it in photographs or on TV.

Bakar told me that before everything happened, people used to come here on desert safaris. They'd spend a week or two doing what we're doing now, walking the dunes or riding camels, camping out overnight with the Berbers in their tents. They came for the silence and the peace, to see the stars and to watch the sun sinking into the sand. He met a lot of people from a lot of places. Sometimes they left behind books as gifts, and that's how he learned to speak so many languages. His father was a guide before him, and his grandfather too.

Did you ever want to be something else? I asked, and he shook his head.

Look around you, he said. What more could I ever want?

Some days when it's really peaceful and not too hot and Tilda's being sort of nice to me, I pretend we're tourists on a desert safari. I try to look at things like I'm seeing them for the first time. I sit on Julep and imagine how it would be fun for someone to ride a camel for a day or two. I run my hands through the sand and try to notice small things like the light or the direction of the breeze or the taste of the dates Bakar shares out for our lunch.

Oh isn't this sky marvelous, I'll say, and if Tilda's in the mood she'll say, yes, quite spectacular this time of year.

It's been ninety-seven days since I left home. I mark a little line in the front of my notebook every sunset so I can keep track. By now my mother and I had planned to be in Mauritania, but we hadn't taken all the details into account. Like how many weeks it would take to find a guide, or the number of nights we couldn't move from where we were because of disturbances in the sand that could only mean desert police. Bakar is very careful. He reads the tracks in the sand every morning and then decides what we'll do. He's been right every time. Except once.

Not every day is a good day and that day was one of them. Tilda had gone to use the Sahara bathroom, as Bakar likes to say. Bakar and I were waiting with Julep. I was practicing some of the Arabic words he'd been teaching me, just simple ones like *sun* and *sky* and *apple*. Suddenly, Tilda was coming toward us, her hands up in the air and a man behind her holding a knife to her throat. He was wearing a blue djellaba like Bakar's but he wasn't a Berber. He spoke a language I didn't understand, shouting at us in a voice thin and rasping like an old man's.

Bakar stood very still and held up his hands too. *Da, da*, he kept saying to the man. *Da, da*.

The man kept shouting, waving the knife. Bakar talked to him in a quiet voice, I think it must have been Russian they were speaking. The man stopped shouting and Bakar started walking toward him, slowly, calmly. I stayed with Julep, my heart racing in my chest, and thinking please, please, please don't let anything happen to Bakar.

When he was standing right in front of the man, Bakar held out his hand. The man started to sob and took his arm away from Tilda's neck. She dropped to her knees and sank into the sand, holding her hand over her mouth. Bakar took the knife from the man, said something softly to him, and pushed it deep into his side. The man didn't even cry out, just looked down to see the blood staining the blue with red, spreading out as it grew. I screamed and Tilda crawled on her hands and knees to get away. The knife was still in Bakar's hand, still in the man's flesh. He took his fingers and held them over Bakar's, gave the knife a twist, and then crumpled into himself like an empty sack.

I was crying and Tilda snapped at me to shut up. Bakar crouched over the man a while and then stood up.

Do not be afraid, Zaria, he said. This man asked to be saved or to die. We could not save him.

He took Julep and started walking. Tilda took me by the hand and the two of us followed. There was nowhere else to go.

I was mad at Bakar, so mad I didn't speak to him for three days. Not a word. He just left me in my silence, didn't try to get me to talk the way my mother used to do when I was in a mood. I lay awake all day while the others slept and tried not to let them hear me cry. I hated what an awful place the world had become. I hated that everything was unknown and scary, like men with knives and fathers who might not be where you left them. I hated that I was alone most of all. On the fourth day of silence, Bakar came and sat beside me. Tilda was curled in a ball next to Julep, who was resting in the sand.

Do you know, he said, that the first humans left Africa thousands and thousands of years ago? They started walking, just like you, only in the opposite direction. Walking all the way to India, to Australia, to Alaska. This is the way of our history and our future—people moving from one place to the next, sometimes bringing life, sometimes taking it away.

He looked at me to make sure I was following, and I nodded.

Zaria, he continued, the journey is made with hope. But it is also dangerous and frightening. Sometimes violent. This is survival. This is how we survive.

He took something out of his pocket and put it in my hands.

Look, he said, what do you see?

I looked at the object, turned it around in my fingers, felt the smoothness and coolness against my hot skin.

It's a rock, I said. A fossil, maybe.

He smiled, you are a clever girl. Look closer, he said.

I held the rock up to my eyes and looked. Then I saw it. A baby! I said.

A baby of stone, Bakar said. It cannot live, but it cannot die. It will be here when you and I and our children's children are long dead, when the world ends or begins again.

It's the most wonderful thing I've ever seen, I said.

Yes, Bakar said. It reminds me that life will always be a mystery.

He took my hand and closed my fingers around the baby.

Please keep it with you, he said, please remember that you are here to survive.

When we are safely across the border and into Mauritania, Bakar will turn around and leave us behind. Tilda and I will make our way south alone, using the jewelry we have left, relying on small kindnesses, hoping for the best. Mauritania, Mali, Côte d'Ivoire. The names are like poems on my tongue, exotic and beautiful, written down in Zaria's Great Adventure in my mother's handwriting. My first journey, maybe my last. But I am here.

We walk on, we brush the sand from our eyes and try to force tears out to soften the sting from the dryness. We share out our small supply of dates and nuts, and drink the water Bakar finds for us in the wells along the way. Sometimes we camp with Berber families, who cook us a hot meal and sit with us around the fire playing music. They ask questions about us that Bakar translates. *Where are you from, where is your family, does your home still exist?* Once, after I had answered all their questions, a little girl who was sitting in her mother's lap came over to me and patted me very gently on the head. Her touch was so tender that I cried.

I'm learning to read the sand like Bakar. I can tell when someone has walked before us, or which direction the wind is taking. Sometimes when it isn't too hot, I take my shoes off and walk barefoot behind Bakar. Blood, tears, bones, the sand takes it all and still it remains as before, just tiny grains that shift softly with the wind. I don't think I'm so scared anymore. I hold the stone baby in my hand and squeeze tightly. I know it won't break.

Oh isn't this sky marvelous, I say, and Bakar, smiling his smile, replies, yes, it is quite spectacular this time of year.